I0580137

MARY CRAWFORD

Soul Scars

HIDDEN HEARTS
PROTECTION UNIT BOOK 3

Copyright

HIDDEN BEAUTY SERIES

Until the Stars Fall from the Sky

So the Heart Can Dance

Joy and Tiers

Love Naturally

Love Seasoned

Love Claimed

If You Knew Me (and other silent musings) (novella)

Jude's Song

The Price of Freedom (novella)

Paths Not Taken

Dreams Change (novella)

Heart Wish (100% charity release)

Tempting Fate

The Letter

The Power of Will

HIDDEN HEARTS SERIES

Identity of the Heart

Sheltered Hearts

Hearts of Jade

Port in the Storm (novella)

Love is More Than Skin Deep

Tough

Rectify

Pieces (a crossover novel)

Hearts Set Free

Freedom (a crossover novel)

The Long Road to Love (novella)

Love and Injustice (Protection Unit)

Out of Thin Air (Protection Unit)

Soul Scars (Protection Unit)

OTHER WORKS:

The Power of Dictation

Vision of the Heart

#AmWriting: A Collection of Letters to Benefit The
Wayne Foundation

DEDICATION

For those who overcome their pasts and win:

Your strength and tenacity are awe inspiring.

CHAPTER ONE

TOBY

"THEY'RE BACK. WE NEED to step up our efforts to stop them."

That simple statement from Tristan is enough to send my blood pressure through the roof.

"What will it take to shut these creeps down?" I ask as I push my laptop away. "I thought Bex Michaels and his wife, Felena Hopner, were on a no-paid vacation behind bars for being pedophiles and scam artists?"

Tristan sighs. "Unfortunately, it's like one of those games at the fair. When we shoot one of them down, another one pops up. We don't know how extensive their human trafficking ring really was. There is no limit to the depths of their depravity."

Depravity. Oh, I know all about the meaning of the word. I was kidnapped and held captive by the queen of depravity for five years. She stole my teenage years from me and did unspeakable things in the name of making me a better person and saving me from my family. I know exactly what these kids are going through. That's why I'm driven to find all those who are lost.

"So, what are we doing to stop it?" I demand more harshly than I intend.

Tristan reaches out and puts his hand on my shoulder. "Look, I understand your passion. That's why I flew you out to Florida. I want you to work with Cody Erickson and his team. Captain Schumaker has made this a priority for his officers. So, with our face recognition technology and complex databases and their personnel, maybe we can team up and truly make a difference this time."

"I hope so. Too many kids are paying the price for apathy and political grandstanding."

"You should know me well enough to know I don't play those kinds of games," Tristan counters.

"I do, otherwise, I wouldn't be here. I would get rich designing mindless video games."

Tristan laughs. "Hey, don't knock that career path. Mindless video games pay the bills and allow me to do this kind of work."

I blush and stare down at the ground. "I always forget about that branch of your business. I stand corrected. Game on!"

As I enter the conference room, everyone greets me like I'm some sort of hero. There is a huge box of donuts in the middle of the table. I've never seen so many types of donuts in one place. I nod toward the box. "Are we celebrating something?"

Cody grins at me. "We sure are! We're celebrating the

arrival of the brainiacs. You guys are the missing piece which will help solidify the team and give us a much-needed boost."

I snicker. "Kissing up much? You do realize I'm only a computer programmer, right? I'm not Chuck Norris. I can't save the day or blow up stuff."

"Well, crap! I miss blowing things up," Cody responds with a dramatic sigh.

"There was the scene the other day at the gas station on the corner of 22nd Avenue —" Pauline suggests.

"Rookie, that doesn't count because I didn't make it blow up. It was caused by a confused teenager who couldn't tell the difference between his clutch and the gas pedal."

Pauline wrinkles her nose at Cody. "You know, you can stop calling me Rookie. There have been at least two more classes of cadets since I was hired. I am no longer the Rookie."

Cody reaches out to affectionately fluff her hair. "Maybe so — but you'll always be *my* Rookie. You might as well get used to it. I will call you 'Rookie' until the day you die."

Pauline rolls her eyes. "Oh great, something to look forward to."

I turn to Cody. "So, why exactly am I here?"

Cody grimaces. "The participants seem to be using a new app we haven't seen before. It allows them to use and shed identities like snakeskin. We can't see them or trace them. They seem to be interchangeable and disposable. We have to figure out how to get into the system and put someone on the inside. We need your help to do that."

I blow out the breath I've been holding. "Just so I understand — you want me to breach a system ... but you don't know what it's called. You want to plant someone on the inside of the system... but you don't want them found. Once inside, you want to use their own system against them to shut them down. Do I have that straight?"

"Pretty much. We also don't want a whole bunch of publicity around this either."

I chuckle softly. "Oh, is that all? I'll get right on it. I'm so glad you didn't ask for anything difficult."

"What are you complaining about? I brought donuts," Cody jokes.

"An exceedingly good choice. Because I'll need all the sugar and caffeine on the planet to reach your goals."

CHAPTER TWO

PAULINE

I AM NOT A schoolgirl. I am not a schoolgirl. I am not a schoolgirl … I mentally chant to remind myself I'm a dignified professional law enforcement agent every time I see Tobias Payne.

He makes me feel as if I'm thirteen years old every time he enters the room. *Oh, my gosh!* The man is devastatingly handsome. Part of his disarming charm is that he doesn't seem to think so. He is shy and self-deprecating, but oh so funny.

Cody clears his throat like he's expecting me to say something. I look at him blankly. He smirks at me. He knows all about my crush on Toby, so he repeats the question as if there's some other reason I didn't hear it properly.

"You were in on the bust of Bex Michaels and later helped with the arrest of his wife for fraud. Did you get a feel for how many layers of leadership there were in his organization?"

I shake my head. "Unfortunately, I was there to rescue the teenagers. I didn't get a chance to talk to anybody except for Bex. He was clearly in charge."

Toby shifts in his seat. "I've talked to one of the victims, Isadora Lopez, quite a few times over the years. She says there didn't seem to be anyone in charge other than Bex Michaels and his wife. He had favorite clients who frequented his business more often than others. It's possible one of them stepped up and took over the business after he went to jail."

Cody grins. "How is Izzy doing?"

"She loves her new job at Hallway Innovations. Will Kordes says she's one of the brightest people he's ever worked with."

"That's great! I wish it was all good news. DeAndre — one of the other victims — is struggling. His time in captivity did a number on him. He's having a hard time with college."

Toby runs his hand through his hair, exposing the gauges in his ears. "I'll touch base with him. Becoming acclimated to the real world after you've been through hell is not an easy process. I wonder if he's still going to counseling. It's hard for guys to admit they need help."

Cody nods. "Thanks. I'm sure his brother, Dashonte, would appreciate you looking in on him."

I lean forward. "You know what really gets me? These perps and johns — they get a slap on the wrist, if anything, and the victims have a lifelong sentence they can't escape. I just wish there was a way we could even the scale."

"That's why Identity Bank has partnered with your agency and the feds. We are trying to shut these guys down for good, so they can't keep popping back up under new identities. We have to do a better job of protecting men, women, and children from becoming victims," Tristan explains.

Toby shakes his head. "I saw a news story the other day. It was about a bunch of politicians and businessmen who were caught up in a sting. They never talked about the actual victims — you know, the prostitutes who were more than likely runaways and abused spouses who were working for pennies if they were paid at all. They never talked about the fact that these people were given drugs to control them. It was all about the poor people who were caught and how their lives and reputations would be destroyed. We need to change the conversation."

I roll my shoulder. "We do — but I am not sure how to reach the people who matter."

Toby nervously pulls on the neckline of his T-shirt. "For many years, I didn't want to talk about what I went through. I was tired of being known as the boy who was kidnapped. I wanted to hide that part of my identity and move on. But maybe I need to talk about all those years I was lost and how I found myself through helping others."

Cody nods. "I've told you before, working with you changed the way I approach reports of missing children and teenagers. I view sexual assault and consent differently in light of our conversations. Even though I go to routine training at the police academy, I'm at a point in my career where I often teach workshops and your experiences have taught me to reevaluate how I determine who a victim is and how I question them. So, Tori and I absolutely believe your story and others like it could change the conversation around child abduction and human trafficking. Contrary to popular belief, it is not a victimless crime."

Toby clears his throat. "In theory, that all sounds great. In reality, I have to develop enough objectivity to tell my story with enough clarity, so it's helpful to other people and not so boring the audience sleeps through it."

Tristan sets his pen down on the table. "Toby, your brother has worked for me for several years. So, I've only heard bits and pieces of your story as you've chosen to share them with me. But the parts I've heard are riveting. Should you choose to share your story to increase awareness for victims, it could be a game-changer. Let me know if you choose to do that. I'll be happy to facilitate it for you. I have the tools to amplify your voice."

Toby cringes. "I'm just getting used to using my voice, I'm not sure if I'm ready to have it amplified."

My hand is sweaty as I knock on the door. I can't believe I'm doing this. Yet, here I am. I even called my mentor, Dylan Palmer, to see if he thought it was a good idea. He told me that I wouldn't know if I didn't give it a shot.

When Toby answers the door, he has a Trisha Sroka novel in his hands. Instantly, I feel guilty for interrupting him. "Any good?" I ask, pointing to the book.

"Yeah, I just started Fires Blaze, but the first one in the series, Fires Fever, was great."

"Oh, that's awesome. I'm always on the lookout for good books. Umm … is it all right if I come in?"

Toby steps back. "Sure. I suppose. How did you know I would be here?"

"Cody told me this is where you stay when you come

to Florida."

Toby closes the door behind us and sets his book down on the coffee table. "Yeah, since my kidnapping, I don't like to stay in a hotel, no matter how nice it is. Since Tori and Cody got married, Tori has been nice enough to sublease this place to Tristan. Phoenix and I stay here whenever we need a place to crash when we come here on business. Sometimes, we're here so often, I feel like I might as well give up my place in Oregon."

Toby points to the refrigerator. "Want something to drink? I've got soda or fancy sparkling water."

"I'm a Pepsi girl."

"I've got that. Ice or no?"

"Ice works, but I can get it."

"My mom would box my ears if I made my company serve themselves."

"Well, since I barged in on you, I'm not sure I count as company."

"Why are you here?" Toby asks as he fills a glass half full of ice and then tops it off with Pepsi. He pours himself a cherry 7-Up and carries them into the living room.

I pull the coupons to the theater out of my pocket and show them to him. "I thought you might want to go see a movie with me."

Toby pales. "I'm sorry. That was really nice of you. I wish I could go — but I don't do movies."

"I promise not to make you watch a silly, mushy chick flick with me. I'm a cop. I like action movies."

Toby sits down on the couch and pats the cushion beside him in an invitation for me to join him.

"I wish it was as simple as a difference in taste — but, that's not it at all. It's difficult for me to explain, but I'll try. You know I was kidnapped when I was twelve, right?"

I nod. "Of course. That's why you're so passionate about trying to help find other missing people. I admire you so much for your courage. I don't know what I would do if I were in your shoes. I might work in a completely different field. I don't know, maybe rescuing manatees or something."

Toby smiles. "The thought occurred to me. When I was held captive for all those years, I used to fantasize about working on a ranch in Texas and riding horses on the open range. I thought it would be great to have a job where I never had to stare at four walls and the ceiling again in my life."

"I can't imagine. I suppose you probably get nauseous when you walk in a room," I sympathize as my stomach suddenly becomes queasy at the thought.

Toby nods. "So, the reason I don't go to movie theaters is somewhat related. The monster who kidnapped me went by the name Rapture Borges. She had me convinced that because my big brother was a soldier and was hunting Osama bin Laden, soldiers would come after my family and she was protecting me. Rapture used to test my loyalty by leaving me alone in the movie theater. One time, I tried to leave, and she blindfolded me and held a knife to my neck. She told me my parents were at home, and there were agents of Osama bin Laden holding them at knifepoint too."

"Oh, how horrible! You must've been terrified."

"In retrospect, it seems idiotic that I believed all her

garbage."

"I studied this in the police academy. I don't know the specifics of your case, but if she did what most kidnappers do, she gained your trust and then she systematically brainwashed you using sleep deprivation, food deprivation and abuse."

"That's exactly what she did. She and I were friends — or at least I thought we were — for several months online before she ever kidnapped me. I had no idea how evil she was until it was far too late. She managed to keep me for five years before Jameson found me. So, I'm sorry to ruin your plans. I still can't bring myself to go to a movie theater. The flashbacks are just too much."

I stick the movie tickets back in my pocket. "It's not a big deal. Really. I only came over to invite you to do something fun because it's the weekend and you're in town with no one to hang with. I figured you'd be bored. If going to the movies is not fun for you, it sort of defeats the purpose. The last thing I want to do is make you feel uncomfortable." I pick my purse up and sling it over my shoulder. "Thanks for the soda. Have a good weekend."

Toby reaches out and puts his hand on my arm. "Wait! Just because I can't go to the movies, it doesn't mean I want you to leave. I'm sure Cody and Tori left something interesting to do around here."

I swallow hard. "This could get interesting."

"I thought you had a sense of adventure?" Toby teases.

"I was referring to actors on a screen. I, personally, am a little more reserved."

"Sometimes, real life is more fun than the movies," Toby says with a wink.

Chapter Three

Toby

CODY KNOCKS ON THE doorframe of my temporary office at Identity Bank, startling me. I glance up at the clock and breathe a sigh of relief. I guess I haven't missed our meeting after all. "Hey, come on in." I greet as I take a stack of files off of the one chair in the office.

"Did Pauline work up enough nerve to touch base with you Friday?"

I nod. "She did. Thanks. We had a great time."

"What did you see? She didn't know what to suggest. I told her to let you decide what movie to see."

I shrug. "Couldn't see a movie. PTSD got in the way."

"Geez, I'm sorry. I should have warned her about that."

"How would you have known? I've never really told anyone before now."

"Still, Dylan and I pushed the rookie out of her comfort zone and encouraged her to ask you out. We put you in a bad situation."

I chuckle. "You guys are as bad as my big brother.

Once you guys got happily paired off, you have to make sure everyone else is too.”

“I may have to plead the fifth,” Cody mumbles.

“No worries. Pauline and I actually had a great time. Those 3D puzzles you have at your house are something else. We spent hours putting one together. I know it sounds like something my grandparents would’ve done, but it was super challenging and more fun than I ever thought it would be.”

“Aren’t they? Ketki got us started on those. When I first started putting them together, I could barely put together a two-dimensional puzzle. Over time, the puzzles became more and more complex. Tori and I had some of the best conversations ever as we were trying to figure out how to put them together.”

“Why didn’t you preserve the puzzles after you completed them? Some of those are works of art.”

Cody shrugs. “I have the very first ultra-complex one we completed on my desk at work. For me, it’s not about the puzzle, it’s about the process we went through to complete it.”

I grab my laptop and jacket. “I guess that could be true for a lot of things. Speaking of puzzles, are you ready to see if we can make any headway on this case?”

Did you all hear Reginald Brennan died in custody?” Cody says as I hook up my laptop to the large projection screen.

“One can only hope his passing was accompanied by

a lot of pain and suffering," Tristan replies.

Cody shakes his head. "Tori says corrections officials told her he died of natural causes. No great movie-like ending where he got the death he deserved."

"For a man who tortured dozens of children and teenagers over the years, that ending was far too polite. How is Savannah handling it?"

"Savannah seems more at peace with the whole situation than Mark. I think Mark would like to kill him all over again and cause substantial pain."

Isaac nods his head in affirmation. "I don't blame him. If someone were to hurt my Rosa that way, they would have to lock me out of the jail to keep me from hurting the perp."

I type notes into the computer before I pull up a graph and display it on the large projection screen. "I don't know if Reggie's death has anything to do with the anomaly in the data or if it's just coincidental. If what I'm seeing is correct, it suggests Bex Michaels' and Reginald Brennan's spheres of influence have converged."

Cody blows out a deep breath. "That's the last thing we need. We thought they might have been working together before. Unfortunately, we couldn't find any evidence to support our theory. Are you saying there's new evidence?"

"If you're asking for a smoking gun, I don't have it yet. I'm still developing the software program to unmask the participants who are switching identities. While we were doing that, Phoenix and I noticed some common patterns in IP addresses. There seems to be some consistent overlap between the two groups."

Pauline grins. "All right! Let's get some search

warrants and get this ball rolling. I'm ready to arrest some bad guys."

"Oh, wait … I didn't mean to give the wrong impression. We're not even close to identifying who these people are with one hundred percent certainty. It's merely enough to raise suspicion and trigger our algorithms."

Pauline pops up from her chair and heads over to the coffee machine. "This is so frustrating. You guys are the best minds in the business with better equipment than Quantico, but we're still flying in the dark. What is it going to take to shut these people down? It feels like we're miles behind them. Every day we sit here twiddling our thumbs, more people are being irreparably damaged."

I drop the control to the projection screen and turn to stare at Pauline. Before I can say a word, Cody addresses her. "Someday, Rookie, I hope you learn to think before you speak."

Wordlessly, Pauline returns to the table and sits down.

Cody pivots his attention back to me. "What do you need from us?"

"Felena Hopner is about to get out of jail. I need permission to monitor her computer and devices to see if it leads us anywhere."

"I'll get right on it," Cody says making a note.

"We may still end up twiddling our thumbs, but at least we have a tangible place to start."

Pauline blushes. "Look, I didn't mean anything personal. Erickson is right. Most of the time, my mouth is way ahead of my brain. This was no exception. I meant no offense."

"I know you didn't. Some days, I just need to toughen up my armor," I respond with what I hope is a socially acceptable smile.

Chapter Four

Pauline

"You know, they make a barrel snake for that kind of thing?" my dad points out as he watches me wipe lubricant off my service weapon. "It would cut down your cleaning time."

"I'm well aware. I just left mine in my locker at work."

"Are you okay, honey? It's not like you to forget things," my mom comments as she looks up from her knitting.

I sigh heavily. "No, I'm not all right. I had a terrible day."

My dad starts examining me. "I heard nothing over the radio. Did you guys have a call go south?"

I cringe. I should've known better than to alarm my dad, a former police officer, like that. "No, it was bad, but not that bad —"

"Oh goodness, did you get yourself put on probation again?" my mom asks with a concerned expression.

I throw up my hands in surrender. "You know what? On second thought, my day wasn't nearly as bad as it could have been. I just embarrassed the heck out of myself again."

"What did I tell you about flirting with the guys? A few of them don't have your same sense of humor. They may not get it. You could find yourself on the wrong end of an expensive lawsuit if you're not careful," my dad advises.

"Daddy! This had nothing to do with flirting. It had everything to do with me engaging my mouth before my brain was fully plugged in."

"Oh, my… what did you say this time?" my mother asks, shaking her head. This is clearly not the first time we've had such a conversation over the years.

"It was awful! I wanted to fall through the floor!"

"Oh, come on, it couldn't have been that bad. Everyone there is used to rookies making mistakes," my dad says, trying to cushion my fall.

"No, Dad, even you would have found this cringe-worthy. You know how impatient I can be? So, I was lamenting the fact that we have all this high-tech equipment donated to us by Identity Bank, but the case still seems to be crawling along at a snail's pace. Then I went on to point out that every day we were wasting, waiting to solve the case, a kid was waiting to be rescued."

"What's so wrong with that? Isn't it true?" my mom asks.

"Oh yeah … technically it's true, and I said nothing wrong. Except I said it right to the face of the guy who is working his butt off to try to help us solve the case and — oh, by the way, he was kidnapped and held hostage for five years. If there's anyone acutely aware of the human cost of police inefficiency, it's Toby Payne. I cannot believe I was such an idiot!"

"Oh, sweetheart, that's unfortunate."

"Unfortunate doesn't cover it. Worse still, Cody Erickson noticed my foot-in-my-mouth moment and called me on it in front of a whole room of colleagues."

"What did Mr. Payne say?"

"I haven't had much of a chance to talk to him. We had to move on with the meeting. At the rate I'm going, I'm not sure I'll ever be brave enough to speak to Toby again."

My dad pins me with a sharp gaze. "I didn't raise you to be a coward."

My spine stiffens as I sit ramrod straight at the censure in his voice. "I know Daddy. I'm working really hard to continue your legacy as one of the best detectives to ever serve the state of Florida. It's just that I think a lot of Tobias Payne. The thought that I hurt him — even inadvertently — is crushing. If he hates me, I'm not sure I want to know."

"I always taught you that information is power. Don't forget that."

"You're right. I'll try to make amends."

I carefully creep into Toby's office and place a large 7-Up on his desk. When I find his office empty, I'm relieved to escape any possibility of awkward conversation, but then disappointment sets in as I realize nothing would be solved this way. I grab a stack of sticky notes and sit down in his chair. Composing a coherent note which will fit on a two–by-three piece of paper is harder than it seems.

I'm concentrating so hard I jump when Toby taps on my shoulder. "Can I help you? I thought our meeting wasn't for like an hour," Toby says as he sets a box of flash drives on his desk.

I flush bright red. "It isn't. I brought you a soda in case you were thirsty as a peace offering and to apologize for my thoughtless remark the other day. You want to go for a walk or something?"

Toby glances up at the clock on his wall. "I suppose I have a few minutes. But I can't take too long. I have to get ready for the meeting."

"Okay, that's fair — especially considering I sprung myself on you. Here's the 7-Up. Enjoy!"

"Umm, thanks. Although I usually drink coffee this time of the morning."

I smack my forehead. "I should have probably guessed."

"Based on what? I never told you what I prefer to drink every minute of the day. You're being way too hard on yourself."

"I've worked with you several times before. I should've paid attention."

"Ah, good point. It's second nature for me. I guess because noticing the little stuff helped me stay alive for so many years, I can't turn it off now. You like Pepsi over Coke, crushed ice as opposed to whole and you usually drink coffee before nine a.m. However, if you've been out on a stakeout, you drink coffee all day. You like your coffee as sweet as a dessert."

"Wow! Are you sure you don't want to apply for work

on the police force as an undercover agent? Your memory is scarily accurate. The only thing you missed is that I like Vanilla Coke — but you wouldn't have any reason to know."

Toby puts his hand at the small of my back as we walk out the front door of Identity Bank and head down the sidewalk.

"I don't think I've ever seen you drink Vanilla Coke."

"How would you know if I was drinking Vanilla Coke? They all look the same."

"They might look the same, but they smell different."

"Okay Smart Aleck, if you know so much about me, what's my favorite color?"

Toby rolls his eyes. "That one isn't even a challenge. Your favorite color is purple."

"How did you know?"

Toby stops walking and turns me toward him. Gently, he removes an ink pen haphazardly stuck in my bun. "You are the only person I know who walks around with a stash of pens with purple ink. Not only that, you stick them in your hair like they're modern art. The pens are kind of hard to miss. The other day, Cody and Dylan had an office pool running to see how many you would stick in your hair before the end of the day."

I snicker. "So, what was your entry into the office pool?"

"I chose a reasonable number of four, but I think the winning bid was seven."

"Okay, like you said that's kind of an obvious one since I wear it all over my sleeve so to speak. What's my favorite flower?"

Toby is silent for so long I wonder if I've somehow crossed the line again with my casual banter. "That's a harder one, for sure. My degree of confidence is not as high with this guess, but based on what I've observed, I would have to say daisies."

"*No freaking way*. Dude! No one ever guesses that because most people like more exotic flowers. How in the world did you know?"

"Well, you doodle a lot with those purple pens of yours and daisies are one of your favorite subjects to doodle. I saw you at my brother's wedding. There were flowers strewn all over the table."

"Yeah, that was one of the most enchanting weddings I've ever seen. The castle cake was perfect, and Kendall's dress was exquisite. I still can't believe Tristan flew a bunch of Jameson's friends there from Florida. I was even more blown away that I got to be one of them. I was still a student at the police academy when Jameson and I first met. He used to practice with me late at night at the local gun range. He's part of the reason I earned top marks at the Academy."

"Yeah, my brother is pretty amazing. Anyway, the reason I know daisies are your favorite flower is because you left all the more expensive flowers on the table and arranged the daisies into a spray and placed it behind your ear. I had official duties to do that night because I was in the wedding party, but I'll have to tell you I could barely keep my eyes off you all night. I was sad when we could only connect for one dance."

"Me too. I'm forever apologizing to you for my mistakes and our missed opportunities. Clearly, you do a better job of paying attention to what's going on in my life than I do. I don't seem to have a clue. It kills me that

I was so rude and insensitive to you in the meeting with all those people present. The thing that gets me is I should know better. I may not know all of your story, but the pieces I do know are absolutely horrific. I shouldn't have said anything. Someday, I'll learn to keep my mouth shut."

"Are you under the impression I'm upset with you because you tripped up over the fact that I was a hostage?"

I nod. "Aren't you? I was pretty rude to you."

Toby shrugs. "I spent years being mad at the world. First, I was mad at Rapture for taking me away from my family and lying to me for all those years. I was angry with myself for not having the courage to run away. I was mad at my family for not being able to find me faster. Honestly, my anger almost killed me. There were times during those five years when I seriously contemplated suicide. I watched videos on the Internet to show me the most effective way to kill myself. I thought about it a lot."

"Oh my gosh! That breaks my heart. Please tell me you don't think that way anymore."

"I don't. But I still struggle with Post Traumatic Stress Disorder and depression. Whenever we handle a case which doesn't end well, I have a raging case of survivor's guilt. It always causes me to wonder why I was so special and different. How in the world did I manage to escape with my life, when others are not so lucky? That's a question I may never get an answer to no matter how much counseling or education I receive. I've spoken to several highly qualified FBI profilers about it. It boils down to the solid coping skills my parents instilled in me, and my ability to instinctively use them until my brother came to rescue me."

"Your story is remarkable. I'm sorry if my words brought back the painful times for you."

"Like I said, it happens all the time. It's just something I have to deal with. Thanks for caring. I'm done being mad at people for saying stupid things. Now, I'm on a mission to change the world, so what happens to me doesn't happen to other people."

CHAPTER FIVE

TOBY

"I DIDN'T KNOW YOU were coming today. Why didn't you say anything? I could've booted up my new game. Although, I'm having trouble making it accessible for my stepdad. Do you think you could help me with coding? When I do the voiceover prompts for visual impairments, it messes up the graphics."

"Ketki, you should probably take a breath in there somewhere," I respond, addressing the tall, willowy teenage gaming enthusiast. "I don't do much gaming programming anymore. I'm woefully out of practice. You are probably a more skilled programmer than I am by a long shot."

Ketki's brows furrow in confusion. "That's not what I heard. Tristan told my stepdad you were one of the most talented programmers he has ever hired. He told John you could solve any programming issue he put in front of you — no matter how complicated."

I blush. "That was nice of him to say. I'm not sure it's true, but it was nice, nonetheless."

"Tristan doesn't lie. I can tell when people lie. He

wasn't lying," Ketki insists, as she stuffs her hands in her pockets. Her spectrum disorder causes her to have unusual hand movements when she's distressed or anxious.

"I didn't mean it that way, Ketki. We simply have a difference of opinion about my skills. I'd be happy to look at your game with you, but I need to talk to your stepmom first if she's around."

"She is in the kitchen with Dad. He's working on a case and she's doing lesson plans."

I cringe. I guess I should've planned ahead. Suddenly, my impromptu idea doesn't sound so hot. "They sound busy. Maybe I should've called first."

"Don't worry about it. They get cranky if they don't take a break now and then. Besides, they like you. It would upset them if they knew you were in town and didn't stop by to visit."

Ketki abruptly takes my hand and leads me to the kitchen. "Mom, look who came to see you," she announces loudly.

Shelby stands up and tucks her blonde hair behind her ears. "Toby! I didn't know you were back in town. Sit down, I'll get you coffee."

"When my mom says she'll get you some coffee, it's like it's from a coffee shop," Ketki confides. "You should see their machine."

Mark grins at me. "My daughter is right. We do coffee fancy around here. You want a latte or something?"

"That works. I've been putting in lots of late nights at work."

"You want sugar?" Shelby asks as she prepares my latte.

"Yeah, quite a bit, please."

"I understand. I've been grading papers, so I get it."

"What brings you by?" Mark asks.

"Shelby, I don't want to interrupt your plans for the day, but I need to talk to you about something that's been bugging me," I blurt.

Mark bristles. "Something bugs you about Shelby?"

The coffee machine makes a loud noise as Shelby blends my drink.

"Did you come here to bully my stepmom?" Ketki asks incredulously.

My eyes widen comically. "No! Absolutely not! I'm doing a terrible job of explaining myself. Nothing bugs me about you. I came here to ask for your advice about a situation that's bothering me. I knew you would probably have the expertise to help me."

Shelby sets a large latte in front of me and sits down at the table. "Perhaps you should start at the beginning. Does this conversation need to be private?" she asks as she looks pointedly at Mark and Ketki.

I shake my head. "I guess not. I should probably get used to having an audience."

"If you're sure, but I'm happy to have a private conversation if you'd like."

"I appreciate that, but that's actually what I'm here to talk to you about. I figured if anybody would understand my struggle, it would probably be you. You know, after everything that happened to me, I didn't want to talk to anyone — even my family. I wanted the universe to forget

I was Tobias Payne, childhood kidnapping survivor."

"I understand. I buried my past so deep it took me years to admit the full truth to myself. If it wasn't for my cancer diagnosis and finding Savannah, it's likely I'd still be in denial about the trauma of growing up homeless and under the influence of a tyrannical abuser."

"How long did it take before you could admit your truth out loud to strangers?"

Shelby chuckles dryly. "Oh, much longer. It's still not the most comfortable thing I do. Why?"

"Well… after years of trying to distance myself from those years, I'm suddenly wondering if that's the right strategy for me. Maybe I should tell my story more often."

"You're not planning to stand in the middle of the parking lot at the grocery store and announce it to people, are you?" Ketki asks.

"No, not exactly. Although I am shy enough, even sharing it at all kind of feels that way," I admit as I take a long drink of my latte.

"I'm not sure I'm following the conversation. Why are you suddenly considering changing your tactics? What has changed?" Mark asks, showing his legal, analytical brain.

"You know I've been working with Identity Bank for years now. Gradually, Tristan has been putting me out in the field with different law enforcement officers. As I work on the front lines of more cases, I keep noticing the same things over and over. Many of these kids are making the same mistakes I made as a kid. I always wonder whether me telling my story could stop a few of these kids from becoming victims."

"If I hadn't been helping the police to catch the people who hurt Aunt Savannah, I might've been the kind of kid they were after. I didn't fit in well at school, I didn't have any good friends and my dad was a single parent who was focused on his job."

"That's a little harsh, Ki, don't you think?" Mark says.

Ketki shrugs. "What? It's all true. They just didn't count on you being a lawyer and teaching me all about the dangers of the Internet first. If you hadn't, I would've been their ideal victim."

Shelby smiles at Mark. "Sorry honey, I have to side with your daughter on this one. We are lucky she knew what to do and she was already working with the police. Otherwise, things could have gone in a whole different direction." Shelby turns toward me. "You know, I work with medically fragile students every day. They spend a great deal of time on social media. They are particularly susceptible to online predators."

I sigh. "I don't even know if what I have to say would change any of that. My story isn't so special — especially these days. Safety information is available everywhere."

Ketki nods. "Yeah, kids can get information in lots of places. But, most kids just Google things or find them on YouTube. If a teacher tells us to look stuff up in a textbook or in a pamphlet, most people ignore that stuff. Why should we listen to something from a grown-up who doesn't understand what it's like to live in today's world?" She looks at her parents and shrugs. "Sorry to be so blunt, but that's the way it is. Most kids my age don't listen to their parents or teachers when it comes to stuff about computers and the Internet. We figure you guys are like dinosaurs and don't know what you're talking about."

"So, how would my experience be any different? I'm still a grown-up," I counter.

"Yeah, but you're not lecturing. You've gone through it and besides, you're much closer to our age."

Mark clears his throat. "Age is an interesting consideration. I see little kids in elementary school carrying around cell phones now. The other day, when I was buying groceries, I saw a kid in the store who couldn't have been more than six with her own smartphone. So, what age should we start targeting these kids?"

My stomach turns. "These pedophiles are sick. Pauline and Cody reported they were involved in a human trafficking bust a couple months ago where the youngest victim was eight."

"Toby, you have to tell these people your story. Maybe not everybody will listen — but maybe some people will," Ketki pleads. "Nobody deserves to be kidnapped and hurt. Not people like you, not people like my Aunt Savannah, nobody! We have to stop them!"

"Ketki, I agree. That's why I'm working so hard with Tristan, Cody, Dylan, Pauline and a bunch of other people. I don't know what else I can do, or how I can be more helpful — but I'll try to figure it out."

"Pauline isn't much older than you, is she?" Shelby asks thoughtfully.

"I'm not really sure. I haven't asked. I assume we are about the same age. Why? What are you thinking?"

"If you guys can work on a curriculum together based on your experiences and hers as a law enforcement officer, we can try it out on my students and get their feedback. They're super honest and used to telling their stories to each other."

"Do you think their parents will be okay with that?"

"I'll be sure to get their permission first. But most of them are okay with the experimental nature of our online program."

"Okay, now I have to get over my colossal case of nerves. Even after all these years, it's hard to tell the whole story. What happened to me is still embarrassing."

"Maybe you're not looking at it from the right angle," Ketki argues. "Most people think what you did was totally kick butt. You not only survived, the bad guy — or woman in your case — actually went to jail. Don't forget that part. You won because you survived and still stayed an awesome person."

"Some days, it's hard to remember I'm so awesome."

"The fact you're willing to share the very painful parts of your life to help prevent other people from going through the same thing tells me my daughter's assessment of your character is one hundred percent spot on. Whether or not you want to accept it, you are awesome. I can't wait until you show the world what we already know," Mark says as he stands up and claps me on the back of the shoulder. "When you and my wife team up, you'll be able to move mountains."

Chapter Six

Pauline

I HOLD MY HAND over my stomach as it churns uncomfortably. Of all the things I wanted to inherit from my senior partners, this was not one of them. I stop by Dylan Palmer's desk and grab an antacid tablet before I go in search of one of my mentors.

I find both Dylan and Cody sitting in Cody's office. "You guys got a minute?"

Dylan nods. "I have a Cold Case Squadron meeting in about an hour."

"I'm avoiding paperwork as usual. What's up, Rookie? You look like you're about ready to toss your cookies. You been visiting the morgue again?"

I shake my head. "Harrison brought in a breaking-and-entering suspect. He needed a female officer to help him take pictures. They suspected she might be hiding evidence in her clothes."

"Uh-huh, sounds like our usual procedure," Cody says.

"Mariah Ikenberry might've been at the B & E, but I don't think that's the real crime here."

"Tell me more," prompts Dylan.

"Ms. Ikenberry presents much more like a victim than a criminal. Her body is covered in bruises, but only where her clothing covers them. She wouldn't look me directly in the eye but seemed relieved when she was taken into custody. She flinched every time my hand came near her body."

"She give her real name?" Cody asks.

I shake my head. "No, ID was confirmed through fingerprints. She said she was Kat Everdeen."

Cody grins. "Nice! I like the ones who read. Where is she from?"

"She's been missing from Alabama for about five months. Her parents are on their way here."

"We have enough to hold her on the B & E?"

"I think so, unless her arraignment is fast-tracked and someone bails her out."

Dylan groans. "How old is she again?"

I double-check the paperwork. "Just turned eighteen two weeks ago."

Cody grimaces. "Does she even want to see her parents?"

"I don't know. I didn't get a chance to ask. As soon as we confirmed her identity with them, they were on their way here. I figured she could use all the help she can get whether or not she's technically of age."

Cody studies me for a moment. "Physical description?"

"She's about an inch shorter than me. She probably weighs fifteen pounds less. Her hair is lighter brown and longer. Why?"

"I'll be right back," Cody says as he leaves his office.

Befuddled, I look to Dylan for answers. "Was it something I said?"

"I long ago stopped trying to figure out Erickson. He'll probably explain in a few minutes."

Cody reenters the office carrying a plastic bag. "Congratulations Lawrence, you are now the good cop. I'll be the bad cop if necessary."

"What's all this?"

"I keep telling you that you are a great cop with solid instincts. If you think there's more to Harrison's collar then meets the eye, there probably is. So, let's go figure it out. Mariah will need a confidant. I don't know of a person better suited for the role than you."

"So, what's in the bag?"

"Just a few items to help start the conversation."

My eyes widen when I peek in the bag. "I have so much to learn," I mumble as I follow Cody out of his office.

Mariah scowls at Cody as we enter the room. "Who are you?"

"Oh, I'm sorry, I didn't introduce myself. I am Cody Erickson. I'm a senior detective."

Mariah turns back to me. "I've been here for hours. I have to take a pee and I'm starving. When are they going to transfer me?"

"Soon, I promise. Detective Erickson just has a few more questions for you."

"How many more questions do I need to answer? I already told you — I had no business being in that lady's house. She had a bunch of really nice boxes outside. I could tell she got a brand-new computer and entertainment system. It was plain as day. So I got tired of not being able to eat. The new stuff sells better at the pawnshop. I figured she wouldn't even have had time to fill out the registration yet. I didn't see an alarm system, so I went for it. I didn't see the built-in alarm on her stupid door knocker. So, her alarm went off as soon as I jimmied the door."

"How did the cops know it was you and not one of your partners?" I ask.

"I was still trying to get my tool out of the doorframe when the police showed up. The camera caught the whole thing on tape. The guy who was supposed to be looking out for me was long gone and I have no idea what happened to the person who planned the whole thing."

"You got a name?" I press.

Mariah smirks. "I don't exactly work with honest, upstanding citizens. What makes you think they'd tell me who they really are? Of course, I don't have real names. Heck, I don't even know who I am anymore."

"We're aware of that, 'Kat Everdeen'. We are trying to help you — but we need you to help us."

"I - I don't know what you're talking about," Mariah stammers.

"Mariah, I took pictures of you. I know you are in incredible pain. Your injuries are not consistent with the actions you described during your B & E. I have a strong hunch you're not a criminal so much as the victim of a series of crimes. Please let us help you."

"Why do you want to help me? You have no idea of all the things that I've done. Dirty things. Awful things. Criminal things. Things my mother would hate me for."

"It doesn't matter. Mariah, please listen. It doesn't matter what you've done. No one deserves to be hurt like you've been hurt. There isn't anything you could have done to deserve those marks on your body."

Mariah sobs. "But … I ran away … I quit school … I took ecstasy."

"Not the best choices you could have made, but still no excuse for anyone to hurt you. Please let us help you."

"Heath was such a liar. I can't believe I bought everything he said."

"Heath? Who's Heath?"

Mariah grabs a tissue from a box sitting on the interrogation table and blows her nose. When she finishes, she takes a couple of deep breaths and continues. "I swear, if I would've taken like five seconds and paid attention to those movies I watched as a teenager on the Lifetime Channel, I could've saved myself a bunch of pain. My life is like one of those movies now. So, I met this guy Heath at a party last summer. One of my girlfriends was dating a college dude. So, I went to a party at a frat house. My friend told me to be careful and not drink anything. I thought she was being lame. So, I blew off her advice. The next morning, I woke up in this guy's bed. He acted real nice like he was protecting me from the other guys. His name is Heath. I feel so stupid because I don't even know his last name or if Heath is even really his name."

Mariah starts to cry again. I get her a bottle of cold water. "It's all right. Take your time."

She shakes her head. "No, I don't want to take my time. I have to get this out before I lose my nerve. Anyway, this Heath dude was like my Prince Charming. He was handsome and attentive. He was super smart and loved books. He was like my dream guy. He was so much more sophisticated than my high school boyfriend. The next thing I knew, he talked me into quitting school and moving with him to Florida because he was transferring schools. He convinced me that it would be super easy to get a GED and start working at my dream job. It seemed logical because my mom had just remarried and didn't have a lot of time to deal with me. Nobody seemed to notice me anyway, so I left."

I hand Mariah a new tissue. "What happened next?"

"Well, you can pretty much guess … There was no job at Sea World as an apprentice animal trainer — even if I did get my GED. We never even got close to Orlando. I doubt that Heath was ever a college student. He probably never even read those books he professed to love."

Mariah studies a bruise on the inside of her elbow.

"At first, it seemed like I hit the lottery. I was with a gorgeous older, college-guy who catered to my every whim. We stayed at luxury hotels and lived like every day was a vacation. It was everything I dreamed my life would be like — until it wasn't."

Mariah takes a gulp of her water. "I'll never forget the first day Heath hit me. I swore it would never happen to me. My real dad used to smack us all the time. That's why my mom divorced him. We moved all the way to

Alabama from Montana to get away from my dad — or as my mom calls him — an unfortunate sperm donor. My whole childhood, I was warned against guys like him. Yet, all of a sudden, I found myself miles away from home in the arms of one."

"How scary for you," I comment.

"No kidding!" Mariah answers. "At first, I tried to justify Heath's behavior. I didn't want to admit I'd made a terrible mistake. I decided it was because Heath and I had been drinking a lot and doing a lot of club drugs. I didn't know it was actually a test to see what I would tolerate. I failed miserably — or I guess you could say I passed with flying colors."

"What do you mean?" I ask.

"As soon as Heath hit me and I didn't leave, my fairytale life ended. He began hitting me every day. Then it got so much worse. First, it started with what he called 'rough sex'. Eventually, he didn't even ask permission. I was so scared."

Mariah tries to rub her bruises away. "I wasn't raised to be the kind of person he was turning me into. During the day, he taught me to pickpocket the tourists. He told me to choose mothers with upscale strollers and nice cars and distract them. If I didn't fleece enough marks in a day, he beat me."

"Is that when the breaking and entering came into the picture?"

Mariah nods. "That wasn't until much later, though. First came Heath's so-called friends."

A shiver goes up Mariah's spine. She stops talking for a moment as she stares blankly at the wall.

Finally, she takes a deep breath and speaks. "I might

as well tell you everything. It's all disgusting anyway. You'll probably lock me up in jail forever. Pretty soon, Heath decided his torture wasn't enough. He started letting his friends come over to our hotel room to rape and torture me too. Sometimes he watched, sometimes not. I'll be honest with you, he often kept me so high I didn't know who was in the room with us. Sometimes it was another chick and occasionally it was more than one guy."

Cody interrupts. "Mariah, did you ever see anybody film these encounters?"

"I don't know. He was so sick in the head, though, chances are, he did. I'm probably all over the Internet for all I know."

"Was Heath getting paid for these sexual encounters?" I ask gently.

Tears slide down Mariah's face. "I followed a guy to Florida so I could train dolphins and I ended up being a prostitute. I'm such a loser."

"No, Mariah, you're not a loser. You were the victim of a human trafficker. We can help you if you let us," I say as I reach out to pat her clenched hands.

She looks at me blankly, "How?"

I pull the bag out from under the table. "For starters, how about a shower and some clean clothes? Sometimes the little things can make a world of difference. While you are doing that, Cody and I will start the search for Heath.

"You guys believe me?" Mariah asks hopefully.

I nod. "We do."

She tears up. "You have no idea what that means to me. Heath said even if I told someone, it wouldn't matter."

"Don't worry. Heath was wrong on many levels and one day it's going to catch up with him," Cody replies with a fierce expression.

CHAPTER SEVEN

TOBY

I've been preparing for this meeting for days. I finally have decent news to give the task force, backed up by solid data. One look at Pauline and all my preparation flies out of my brain as if it was never there.

Before I say anything, Dylan addresses Pauline. "You okay, Rookie? Need some coffee?"

Pauline shakes her head. Although she usually has beautiful porcelain skin, she is ghost white. Her brown eyes are missing their usual sparkle. She looks like she hasn't slept in days. Usually, when they tease her, she is quick to respond with a smile and a joke in return. Today, Dylan and Cody haven't been able to elicit so much as a smile.

Cody sighs and turns his attention to the presentation screen. "What do you have for us today, Toby? Please tell us you have good news. Lord knows, we could use some around here."

I bring up the first slide. "Actually, I do have a little good news. Without completely geeking you out on computer speak, Phoenix and I have made significant progress on our program to help track and unmask the online predators participating in the human trafficking ring."

"Well, hallelujah!" Dylan responds. "I bet the new technology will help the Cold Case Squadron too."

"I suspect it will. However, there is some bad news involved in this."

"Isn't there always?" Pauline mumbles.

"Don't mind her, she forgot to eat her Wheaties for breakfast. So, what's the bad news?" Cody asks.

"Well, from a law enforcement perspective, we were hoping these cases were localized, but we found that our perpetrators are located across several states and they seem to be targeting victims as young as ten."

Pauline's head whips up, and she stares at me. "Finding them is not enough. Ten years old? Are you kidding me? We have to stop these guys! Tracking them on the computer won't accomplish anything. We have to stop them before they hurt these girls!"

"Or boys," I pointedly correct.

Pauline looks chagrined. "We have to find these kids before they get hurt. Let me tell you, it's horrific to speak to one of the victims after the fact."

"It's horrific to be one too," I reply softly.

"Oh my gosh! I did not just do that again." Pauline exclaims as she buries her face in her hands. "I am so sorry. That's not what I meant at all. I am just frustrated because it seems like we're losing the war and I don't know how to stop it. I know you're working super hard. It's just that I spent hours at the hospital with a victim. I had to hold her hand while they took pictures and hair samples. Her mom was beside herself. I made promises I never make about trying to get justice for her daughter. Unfortunately, I know there is no justice for what happened to her. Her life will never be the same."

"Pauline, you can't keep score like that. You'll burn yourself out," Dylan advises.

"Says the man who pops antacids like they are M & Ms."

Dylan grimaces as he rubs his stomach. "Exactly. That's why you should do as I say, not as I do."

Cody leans forward. "Seriously, Palmer is right. You have to measure your job performance against another scale. Did you do your best? Were you kind and compassionate? Did you try to find the truth?"

"What if you can't do all those at the same time?" Pauline asks.

"That's the balancing act which makes our job so hard."

"Rookie, it's difficult not to get invested in each victim and each case. Every one of us here has a case which has gotten under our skin even though we know better. Sometimes, it's impossible to draw the line between caring enough and caring too much. But, you can't let your emotions get in the way of doing your job. I know the fight seems overwhelming, but we chip away at it one clue at a time, one lead at a time, one arrest at a time, one conviction at a time until we make a difference. It's all we can do."

"What if it's not enough?" Pauline asks.

"Then you have to let it go and do better the next day."

I clear my throat. "It's important to remember that how you found your victim isn't where she'll always be. She might be in a terrible place right now. But that pain doesn't last forever. With any luck, she'll get stronger, tougher and more resilient. It's hard work, but even nightmares can be the building blocks for a better life."

Pauline sits up straighter in her chair. "You're right. What you're saying is although it may seem like we're losing the war, it's merely a temporary setback?"

"That's the way I like to look at it. If I didn't, it would be too hard to continue the fight," I admit.

"Okay, let me tell you all that I found out from my latest victim. I don't even know if it fits our current case. But it might —" Pauline replies as she pulls a file out of her stack

I'm so far outside my comfort zone, I'm not even sure we're in the same ZIP Code. I'm willing my hands not to shake as I clutch a bouquet and knock on Pauline's door. I have a new respect for her for making the first move a few weeks back. This dating stuff is hard!

The sound of the knocker seems to echo throughout the quiet residential street. Just before I knock again, the door swings wide open and an older gentleman greets me with a welcoming smile. He is walking with a forearm crutch and one arm is held close to his chest. He braces his weight and lets his crutch dangle as he extends his hand for me to shake. "You must be Pauline's young man. I'm Desmond Lawrence, but you can call me Des. My wife Christie is around here somewhere."

"Nice to meet you, sir," I reply. "Is Pauline here?"

"Did she know you were coming, son? She's had a mighty tough day. She's taking a shower and trying to put the day behind her."

I show him the bouquet of daisies. "I know all about her difficult day. That's why I'm here. I was trying to surprise her — I guess I didn't think that through very well."

A woman with thick dark hair comes around the corner. She has an apron on and gardening gloves. There is a smear of dirt across her face. When she sees the flowers, her face lights up. "Oh my gosh! Did you bring those for Pauline? She'll love them! Most women are partial to roses or tulips, but not our little girl. She's always loved daisies and dandelions. I like to call her our wildflower child. She's tough like that. No pampered growing environments for her. Just plant her wherever. Give her a little love and attention and she'll thrive."

"That's a lot of information the young man didn't need to know about our daughter," Des warns, shaking his head in dismay.

"Why ever not? We all know Pauline can be a bundle of contradictions, especially when she's in a 'mood'. I'm just trying to help the boy."

"I appreciate it. Dating can be tricky."

"Do you do a lot of dating?" Desmond asks sharply.

"No, not much. I'm pretty shy."

"Yet my daughter has caught your attention?" he presses.

I blush. "Pauline is funny and brilliant. She's beautiful and compassionate. We have a great time together. She doesn't seem to notice that sometimes I have a hard time putting together a coherent sentence."

"If I know our girl, she probably talks rings around you. She can sometimes be a chatterbox when she's nervous," Mrs. Lawrence adds.

From behind me, I hear Pauline groan. "Thanks a lot, Mom! You want to tell Toby any more secrets while I stand here and watch?"

Pauline's mom shrugs. "No dear, your father already told me I shouldn't be doing that. However, Toby seems like a delightful young man. Look, he brought you your favorite flowers. You should put those in water before they wilt."

Pauline's eyes fill up with tears. "You brought me flowers? Not just any flowers — my favorite flowers? It's not my birthday. We haven't officially been dating long enough to have an anniversary. It's not Valentine's Day or any other holiday that I'm aware of. That means you brought me flowers just because."

I nod. "It seemed like you were having a rough day. I figured these would make you feel a little better."

"Why? I insulted you again today. If anyone should get flowers, it's you. I should be groveling at your feet — not the other way around."

"You've phrased things differently than I might've. But then again, my experiences in life are different from yours."

"You are being way too nice. I basically suggested that boys couldn't be victims of sexual assault. I freakin' know better. Not only do I know the stats, I've helped rescue victims of human trafficking. I've been in on the busts! I practically lost my job over one because I jumped the gun and didn't get backup. So, once again my mouth got in gear way before my brain did."

"I won't argue with you. You shouldn't have said it, but you caught your mistake right away and you apologized. We were having a crappy day. I've been through those exams and the police interviews afterward. They're grueling. I can't imagine what it would be like to have to be on your end of conducting one. I'm sorry you had to be part of that. I wish we could catch all these creeps and get them off the streets, so it wasn't part of your job."

Pauline hands her mom the flowers. "Can you find the right vase for these? I can't remember where you put them all."

"Sure, honey, I'd be glad to. They sure are beautiful. Your man definitely knows what makes you happy."

Pauline walks up and puts her arms around my neck. She steps closer and gives me a tight hug. "I have no idea how you knew I needed those flowers today. But it's the best thing to happen all day. Thank you so much." As she pulls away, she brushes a kiss across my cheek. "I am so lucky to have you in my life."

Desmond clears his throat and says to his wife, "Christie, I forgot you told me you needed potting soil and fertilizer from the garden center. We better go get your stuff. They're closing in a few minutes."

She looks flustered. "I do? I don't remember telling you that."

Desmond tilts his head toward Pauline and me. "Don't you remember, you said something the other day. Don't you need some bigger pots too?"

Suddenly, it's like a light bulb goes on over her head

and she grins widely. "Oh, oh! I guess you're right. I need a bunch of stuff from the gardening center right away. It won't wait until tomorrow. I guess we should go right now!"

Pauline leaves my arms and walks over to the sink, grabs a paper towel, gets it wet, and brings it back over to her mother. "If you're going to go to such great lengths to ditch me here with Toby, you might want to wash your face first, you look like you've been rolling in the mud."

Christie takes the towel from Pauline and delicately dabs at her face. "You act like I don't need to go to the garden center or something —"

"You guys, it's not like I don't appreciate it, but there's definitely a little 'or something' afoot here."

Mr. Lawrence winks at me. "My daughter gets her detective skills from me."

Pauline is snuggled up against my side under a quilt on an old-fashioned porch swing. I'm gently rocking with one foot. "You want to talk about what happened today?"

I feel her take a deep breath and let it out. "This is just between us, right?"

I nod. "Of course. I'm here as your friend, not as your teammate on the task force."

"Thank goodness. Sometimes it sucks to be a phenom."

"I know."

"You know, I'm the youngest detective our department has ever had. Half the people scream nepotism even though my dad worked for a different county. I started with the Explorer program as soon as I turned thirteen. I've lived and breathed police work since I was old enough to understand what my dad did. He used to sanitize cases for me and let me help him solve them when I was just a little kid. I grew up thinking like a cop. I've never known anything else."

"It was like that with me and computers. I learned how to program them because I was bored. I taught myself with library books when I was a young kid. I don't remember not knowing how."

"So you get it. Until now I've been kind of treated like the bright kid cop on the edges of cases. I had a case a while back where I acted super impulsively and almost got fired because I didn't get backup in place first. I acted on my gut instincts. I saved a bunch of kids from a human trafficker."

"I know. I've met with some of the people you saved. Your methods gave me a heart attack, but it was a gutsy call."

"Anyway, I've been trying to keep my head down and do my job. I don't want to give Dylan and Cody any grief because they stuck up for me and helped me keep my job after I royally screwed up. Lately, they've been giving me more responsibility because, like I said, I'm not technically the rookie anymore."

"From what I can see, everyone is happy with your work."

"Yeah, except for the times I randomly stick my foot in my mouth like I've done almost every day I've interacted with you."

I grin and hug her closer. "What can I say? I guess I just bring out the worst in you." On impulse, I brush a light kiss across her lips. *Hmm, it's not as awful as I remember.* I push the thought back as I watch Pauline closely.

Pauline blushes and mouths, "Wow!" before lays her head on my chest. "You definitely push my buttons, that's for sure."

"So what happened on this case?"

"Harrison brought in a suspect. He needed a female officer to do a search. Apparently, I was the only one available, so they called me. When you're a rookie cop — even when you're not truly a rookie — you can get called in for strange stuff. So, I went in to help Harrison. But, I noticed right away this suspect looked like she had been beaten repeatedly. She was covered head-to-toe in bruises — not only new bruises but old ones too. I was upset because Harrison didn't seem to notice. He was too focused on his B & E. The suspect completely shut down around Harrison. She wouldn't talk to him at all, but she opened up to me. Eventually, he caught on and left the questioning to me."

"Smart move."

"I've never felt so far out of my league in my life. This is the first time I've been in charge of questioning — like this wasn't an exercise in the academy. This was somebody's life and she was telling me horrific things."

"I'm sorry, it must've been hard."

"You know what I was thinking the whole time she was talking — besides me not wanting to screw the whole interview up?"

"No, what were you thinking?"

"My overwhelming thought was, 'but for the grace of God go I'. My dad had to retire from his job early. It was catastrophic and he almost died when he was shot. For a long time, it wasn't clear whether my dad would live or die. Then it wasn't clear whether he would walk or use the left side of his body again. My dad was a very angry man when his career abruptly ended. Unfortunately, he took it out on mom and me. Our house was not a very happy place to be for a while."

"Oh man, I can't even imagine what it takes to recover from something like that."

"It's even worse when you stack a moody teenager on top of a man who has lost his career and identity. Of course, all I ever wanted to be was a police detective like my dad. He was hearing none of it because he didn't want me to be in the line of fire — quite literally. We had many epic screaming matches. During those years, I often thought about running away. I wrote countless notes threatening to do just that."

"Wow!"

"Wow is right. I came precariously close to the same path as my victim. I could've made the same choices as she did. There's nothing to say I would've been any more street smart than she was. We've already established I tend to be impulsive and impatient — that's with extensive police training and college courses under my belt. Can you imagine how reckless I would've been without the benefit of my education and training? It would've been a nightmare. I would've been ripe pickings for predators."

"Maybe you're being too hard on yourself. I've seen you work through problems. You are fantastic at thinking on your feet. I suspect you were the same way as a teenager."

"I think you're giving me far too much credit. Even today, there is a part of me who worries about how others perceive me and how I fit in. That would've been lethal in the world of human trafficking."

"So, what's done is done. You can't go back and think about the decisions you could've or should've made. Give yourself credit for the things you did well. It sounds like you have a great relationship with this suspect who actually is a victim. Now we have to figure out how to use it to our advantage to help catch the real bad guys."

CHAPTER EIGHT

PAULINE

"It's a fantastic idea, I swear!" I insist as I sit across Dylan and Cody in Dylan's office.

"Why should we dangle you as bait when we don't even know who all the players are yet?"

"What better way to flush out all the players than to have me on the inside? I can feed you intel a lot faster than you could get it from the outside."

"Why you as opposed to a confidential informant?" Dylan presses.

"You know CI's flake off if they find someone else who will pay them more money. I would never do that. Also, I won't be strung out on drugs or alcohol. You can count on me to give you accurate information."

"Who will keep you safe if you're on the inside? As far as I know, no other agency has agents embedded in either organization that we've identified as potential targets," Cody reasons.

"I'm not completely defenseless, I graduated the top of my class in hand-to-hand combat."

"Hand-to-hand combat isn't any good against bullets

if they find out you double-crossed them," Cody responds with a frown.

"Do you have a better plan?" I growl in frustration.

"Yes, we could wait for Phoenix and Toby to finish developing their software. That should give us live or near-live tracking."

"Watching computer blips on mapping software is not the same as real-time human intel. Do you want to find the creeps who hurt Mariah or not?"

"I do, but I'm not willing to sacrifice you in the process," Cody responds.

"Relax! Toby's refining his program so much that soon he'll be able to tell when the bad guys fart. He'll be able to keep me safe."

Dylan chuckles. "Toby's good, but even he isn't that good. He would be the first to admit his technology isn't ready to be put under that much stress yet. They are still in the early stages of testing."

"Arghh! This is all taking forever! I feel like I should be doing more."

"Seems to me you've done quite a bit to be a positive influence in Mariah's life. The homeowner elected not to press charges against her. You got her a job in the bakery at Tough Break."

"I'm not so sure Mariah's mom thinks that's such a positive development. Mona wanted her daughter to come home. The job at the bakery is perfect though because Mariah can work behind the scenes during early hours without worrying about who she might run across. Mariah's emotions are too raw to face her mom yet."

"That's too bad. I know relationships between moms

and daughters can be tricky — even under the best of circumstances," Dylan says as he glances over at a picture of his fiancé, Lauren, on his desk.

I look up at the clock on the wall. "I need to go. I have an appointment with Casey and Savannah. We're meeting with Mariah at the new Florida headquarters of Uncommon Paths. I'm hoping they can help her get back in school and get the specialized counseling she needs."

"I forgot Casey started his youth outreach program here. That's a great idea Lawrence — unless Mariah is too old to be served."

Cody elbows Dylan. "Remember the first time you met Casey Moore? You thought he was the bad guy. How wrong you were!" Cody snickers.

The tips of Dylan's ears turn red. "Yep, I called that one wrong. You have to admit, on paper Casey's past looked downright sketchy."

I nod. "Casey told me about what he went through. He shared Savannah's story too. That's what makes them perfect to work with Mariah. Hopefully, she'll understand no one is perfect and everyone makes mistakes, but it's possible to move beyond what happened to her. Mariah is still blaming herself like she did something wrong. I hope Savannah's story will help her understand she was the victim of a crime and that it doesn't mean she is a bad person."

"It's something crime victims can't hear enough," Dylan says. "Remember, you're not a bad cop either if you can't solve all Mariah's issues. I know you're trying to be helpful, but sometimes it's out of the scope of our jobs."

"I get that. But right now, I'm the only person she

trusts in the whole state of Florida. I have to try my best."

"I understand that too. But, don't let one victim make you lose sight of the big picture."

When I hear the tumblers turn on the series of locks on the door, I breathe a sigh of relief. At least Mariah is observing the safety protocols we put in place. When she opens the door, I blink in shock. "Where did all your hair go?"

She slumps. "You hate it, don't you?"

"No, actually. It's fantastic! I wish I was brave enough to do something like that with my hair. I dig the purple. It reminds me of my friend Jade's hair — although, I think her streak is hot pink at the moment."

Mariah giggles. "It should. Jade and her mom are the ones who did it all for me. Did you know Diamond could cut hair? I had no idea!"

I shrug. "Me neither — but Diamond has always seemed magical, so I'm not surprised."

"I wanted to get a tattoo, but Jade told me I should wait until things settle down a bit. She doesn't want me to regret my decision later."

"That's probably wise. Tattoos are a giant commitment."

Mariah runs her fingers through her short-cropped hair. "I guess there's no danger of Heath recognizing me now."

"You look amazing. I think your own mother would look twice."

To my horror, tears sprang to Mariah's eyes. "Yeah, for lots of reasons. My mom would be so disappointed in me if she knew the person I am today."

"Mariah, I don't think that's true. I met your mom. She was very concerned."

"She doesn't know all the things I've done. I'm awful!"

"Do you realize the things Heath made you do are not who you are, right? You were tortured and coerced. You didn't do those things by choice. It's not the same thing."

"Why didn't I ask for help? I wasn't a little kid. It's not like I didn't have a voice. So, why didn't I use it? I was an honors student! I had scholarships waiting for me to go to college. Why did I throw it all away? Why wasn't I smart enough to get out of the situation I was in? Why was I dumb enough to get in the crisis to begin with?"

"I could give you some sort of canned answer I was trained to give you as a police officer. But I respect our relationship too much to give you lip service. So, I'll tell you the truth. Personally, I don't know the right answers to your questions. I could guess based on my education and training, but that wouldn't help you much. But, I have three friends who have been through something similar to what you've faced. Would you feel comfortable talking to them?"

Mariah's jaw goes slack. "You're not much older than me. How could you have so many friends who've gone through the same thing as me? What do you do, collect them?"

I shrug. "It's more common than you think. Besides, my dad is a retired cop. I've been hanging around police officers for as long as I can remember. It's an occupational hazard."

"What's an occupational hazard?"

"Knowing people who have had more than their share of bumps and bruises in life."

"I thought you'd be jaded and figure everybody was guilty just by looking at 'em."

"Some people are, I guess. Experience has taught me otherwise. My dad was almost killed by someone who was supposed to be the good guy. His life was saved by the guy he was helping to arrest. It sorta changes your perspective. These days, I try not to assume anything about a person until I know all the facts."

"Is that why you knew to look beyond the surface to see what was really going on with me?"

"I suppose so. I have awesome mentors who have taught me to trust my gut. My gut told me there was more to the story than a jimmied lock. Turns out I was right."

"Yeah, you found a whore —" Mariah says as her face contorts with disgust.

"No, I did not find a whore. I found a crime victim who needs a little help to find herself again. Are you ready to go meet the people who can help you start?"

Mariah tearfully nods. "I hate the person I am now. I want to be able to look in the mirror and not want to throw up when I see my reflection."

As soon as we enter Uncommon Paths, Mariah's posture becomes hostile. I'm curious about her reaction to the open, airy recreation room which contains pool tables, video games, art stations and couches with tall bookcases overflowing with books.

Casey comes over and greets us. "Hi, welcome to Uncommon Paths, I'm Casey Moore."

Mariah zones in on the artwork on Casey's arms. "Jade do that?"

Casey nods. "She sure did. She had to cover some of my earlier bad choices."

"Are you one of Pauline's friends who was kidnapped by human traffickers?" Mariah blurts.

Casey shakes his head. "No, my story is a little different. My dad was addicted to cocaine, so I ran away from home. I spent years on the street. Some of my best friends had that happen to them, though."

Mariah gestures toward all the kids hanging around the great room. "So, what do you do? Round up a bunch of kids and force them to confess their deep dark secrets so you can get insurance money?"

I bristle and start to say something, but Casey holds up his hand to stop me.

"It's a fair question. People who get help from Uncommon Paths are here because they want to be. Nobody will force you to do anything."

Mariah raises an eyebrow. "So basically this is like a free summer camp for troubled kids who have been through hell?"

"Oh, I didn't say it was free. If you want help from us, you have to work for it."

"Yeah, I knew there was a catch. Nobody gives a crap about me. I ruined my life the second I fell for Heath's line of bull."

Savannah comes up behind Casey. "What my husband isn't explaining very well is Uncommon Paths will help you find a way to accept the person you've become and your new normal. When you care about yourself, you'll be able to work through your demons and turn your life around."

"What kind of feel-good mumbo-jumbo is that? What do you know about this stuff? I suppose you were held captive by some deranged kidnapper or something?"

Savannah takes Mariah by the hand and leads her over to a small loveseat behind the desk. She sits beside her. Casey walks over and stands beside his wife in a silent show of support. Savannah takes a deep breath and blows it out before she says, "Actually, that's exactly what happened. After a childhood I wouldn't wish on my worst enemy, I found myself alone on the streets. I figured since I'd been homeless I could fend for myself. I did for a while until I got sick. I trusted the wrong people to take care of me. At first, it seemed like they were going to."

"They?" Mariah whispers.

"What seemed like a really nice husband and wife took me in and got me medical care. They bought me clothes and makeup. When I told them I liked to draw, they got me art supplies and books. I thought for once in my life, I had found a safe place to live. I was wrong. Soon, the woman I looked at as a mother figure and counted on to keep me safe drugged me and stood by as her husband routinely raped me."

Mariah gasps. "Oh no."

"I thought my life couldn't get much worse, but again, I was wrong. The Brennan's tired of me, so they pretended I was a virgin and sold me to another predator. That man chained me to a bed and systematically raped me for years."

"Did you ever feel guilty that you fell into their trap and didn't get away?" Mariah asks in a broken voice.

Savannah nods. "For years, I hid my dirty secret. I thought there was something wrong with me. I assumed I must've done something terrible to deserve the treatment I got. Nothing could have been further from the truth."

"How did you figure out the truth?"

Savannah reaches out and grabs Casey's hand. "Honestly, at first, I had to borrow strength from someone else until I found my own. Casey believed in me and didn't judge me by my past. He simply listened as I told my story. Eventually, I told my story in court and put my perpetrators in jail. Now, I help other people who need to find their inner strength. It's kind of a circle-of-life thing for me."

"If I want to join the program at Uncommon Paths, what would I have to do? I have a job at Tough Breaks. I just started a couple weeks ago, but I like working there. I don't want to stop."

Casey grins. "You're kidding! This is like serendipity."

"What's like serendipity?" Mariah asks, looking thoroughly confused.

"I used to own Tough Breaks. It was my shop before I sold it to go to school to become a counselor. Natalie was my barista."

Mariah swings her gaze around to me. "Is he messing with me?"

I shake my head. "Nope. My dad and I used to have coffee there all the time when I was in high school. Casey had the coolest collection of antique toys I've ever seen."

"That's where Casey and I met. I was just minding my own business, trying to feed my caffeine addiction. But, this guy wouldn't let me be the mysterious new business owner with no friends. He wormed his way into my life and became my confidant. He even used his friends and a big old dog to help me find myself."

"Are you saying I shouldn't trust him?" Mariah asks skeptically.

"No, actually I'm saying the opposite. I never felt safe until Casey Moore came into my life. He has had my back since the moment we met. He helped me find an inner strength I never knew I had. Together, we faced down the monsters who haunted my dreams. If Casey Moore says he's on your side, you can count on him. He'll be the best friend you've ever known."

"Good, I need some friends. I forgot what that feels like."

"Don't worry, we'll help you remember," Savannah replies with a soft smile.

"I have one more question," Mariah adds tentatively.

"Shoot, we like questions around here," Casey replies.

"Do you think it's too late for me to finish high school and go to college? Before my grandpa died, I promised him I would go to school. I was an honor student before I blew it. I had scholarships and everything. Now, I have nothing. He would be so disappointed —"

Casey points to a framed diploma on the wall. "See

that over there? It's mine. The ink on it is probably still wet."

Mariah giggles. "Seriously?"

Casey nods. "I work in a place like this because of a lady named Roberta. A lifetime ago, in California, I sat on a couch very similar to the one you're sitting on. I was trying to put my life back together after one of my friends died of an overdose. I was wrongfully accused of killing her. Fortunately, Roberta helped me turn my life around and learn the restaurant industry from the ground up. I had messed my life up about every way possible, but Roberta still believed in me. It's because of that faith, and the fact that my wife believed I can do anything, I was able to go back to school and reach a lifelong dream. If I can do it, you sure can."

Mariah glances over at me and grins shyly. "I had my doubts about your friends. Especially after I saw this place. It looked too good to be true. But since I trust you, I'll give it a shot. If they have half as much belief in me as they have in each other, I can't help but succeed."

Chapter Nine

Toby

Lines of code are swimming in my head. There's a glitch somewhere. The databases are spitting out garbage code and I can't find the anomaly. I swear I haven't had this much trouble coding since I was about twelve. I don't know what my problem is. Maybe it's simply focus. I find my thoughts are wondering to a willowy detective with sparkling brown eyes and a quick smile. Just as I'm about to dive into troubleshooting mode again, there's a knock on my office door.

I look up expecting to find Phoenix or Tristan, so I'm surprised when I see Cody Erickson. "I know I tend to lose track of time, but I'm pretty sure our meeting isn't until tomorrow."

"It's not, but I didn't figure you wanted to wait for this information."

"What information?"

"Did you know the Brennan's had a son?"

"No, did you?"

"Not until the obituary was printed in the paper. Apparently, there's an Oscar Brennan. He's been staying with an aunt in New Jersey."

"Why do I have a feeling there's more to the story?" I ask.

"I wouldn't have come all the way over here if there wasn't."

"Okay, don't keep me in suspense. What's the big news?"

"We've already established Bex Michaels' marriage didn't seem to survive incarceration so well. We couldn't determine if it was merely a ploy for Felena to get her kids back after she was released from prison or if they actually split up. However, Ms. Hopner was in a prison romance with a civilian on the outside. Care to guess who she hooked up with?"

I shake my head. "I wish I could say I'm surprised, but somehow these lowlifes seem to find each other. I've heard of passing down a family legacy. Somehow, I always envisioned it to be something much more grand than a criminal enterprise catering to pedophiles."

"If you don't have any morals or ethics, I suppose there's a lot of money in it," Cody replies with a sour expression.

"Yeah, if you want to destroy lives."

Cody rolls his eyes. "Inconsequential details to these guys. Apparently, they don't even care about their own kids — let alone someone else's."

"So, now that we have names, how do we change our approach?"

"Unfortunately, we still don't have probable cause to get a search warrant for Oscar Brennan. Being related to bad and evil people and pursuing a relationship with a felon isn't enough. The good news is that we were able to get the search warrants for Felena Hopner' devices and we can track her in real-time. Hopefully, that will lead us to Oscar Brennan's headquarters."

"It might be a good idea to show a few pictures to Izzy and Mariah to see if they recognize anyone. Who knows how long Oscar has actually been in the picture?"

"You're right. I'll reach out to them. They could have some valuable information."

"Let's hope somebody does. This case is frustrating the heck out of me."

I try not to tap my foot as I wait for the microwave to finish heating my lunch. It's unusual for anything at Identity Bank to be less than the latest and greatest. I wonder if Tristan knows it's on the fritz. I laugh at my own nerve. My boss is one of the richest people in the United States. He owns one of the most innovative tech firms on the planet, specializing in both identity protection and fraud prevention software as well as a whole separate gaming branch, which independently brings in millions of dollars. He does not have time to worry about one small malfunctioning kitchen appliance in the break room.

I jump when the man himself peeks his head around the corner. He grimaces when he sees where I'm standing. "I thought they replaced that thing weeks ago. It hasn't worked right since one of the interns tried to heat a burrito in a foil wrapper. Anyway, I came to tell you there's somebody here to see you."

"Not to be nosy or anything, but don't you have office staff for that kind of thing?"

Tristan laughs. "Normally I do. But today they are all at a surprise baby shower for my executive assistant. Fun times. Surprisingly, I was expressly uninvited. I guess my gifts tend to be a little on the extravagant side, and I make everyone else feel bad."

"I can see how that could happen. Didn't you offer to buy your sister-in-law a tire store when she got a flat?"

"Okay, in my defense there was a little more to the story. Ivy had a cute little import she loved. Tires for that thing were hard to find. So, I told her it would be cheaper for me to buy her the whole store. I guess you had to be there, but it was funny."

"Still, most people give cute jammies and a toy or two — not a college scholarship to pay for Harvard. It's a little intimidating."

"I concede you probably have a point."

The microwave finally beeps and I remove my food. When I test it, it's ice cold. I sigh in frustration. "This is absolutely consistent with how my day is going. I don't have time to deal with this right now. I have to go meet whoever's here," I say as I scoop up my TV dinner and throw it in the trash on my way out of the break room.

My stomach growls and I frown. *Geez! Could this day get any longer?* I walk down the long hallway to the lobby and I'm surprised when I come face-to-face with Pauline.

"What are you doing here?" I blurt.

Pauline shoots me a quizzical look and looks over her shoulder. "You asked us to come."

It's only then I notice the thin teenager with the brightly colored hair sitting behind Pauline with her nose buried in a book.

"I did?" I answer, then suggest, "Let's go back to my office."

Pauline smirks and pulls out her cell phone. "You've been working way too hard. Did you forget you sent me this?" she replies as she shows me a text message. She motions for the young lady to follow us.

"Oh, I see. Somebody misunderstood what Cody said. Cody needs to talk to Mariah and Izzy about IDing a couple of potential suspects. It looks like somebody somewhere got their wires crossed when they sent out the message. Let me send him a text message and let him know you're here."

"Well, that could be interesting. Doesn't Izzy live in Oregon now?"

I pull my phone out of my pocket and text Cody the information. When I finish, I gesture toward myself and answer Pauline's question, "Tristan never seems to have an issue with geography. For him, it's merely another excuse to use his plane. In case you forgot, technically I still live in Oregon too."

Pauline's bottom lip slides out. "Actually, you'd be surprised how often I forget. Anyway, this is Mariah Ikenberry. I guess Cody wants to talk to her about the case."

When we reach my office, my stomach audibly growls. To cover the awkwardness, I turn on the extra lamps and close my office door. My stomach growls even louder this time.

Mariah looks at me in surprise as she covers her

laugh with her hand. "Dude, are you okay?"

I motion toward the vinyl chairs in my office. "Please have a seat. Yeah, I … uh … had difficulties with the microwave, so I skipped lunch today. Hi, I'm Toby Payne. I'm working on the task force with Cody and Pauline to help end human trafficking cases like yours. Nice to meet you."

Mariah pales. "I know who you are! I was only a little kid when you were taken, but my mom wouldn't let me go to the library by myself ever again after she heard about your case." She turns to Pauline. "You didn't tell me one of the people you knew who was kidnapped was famous!"

I fidget uncomfortably in my computer chair as my face heats. "I'm not really famous. I was just gone for a long time and the woman who took me was bat-flip crazy. It made for good TV and the networks liked to cover it. I'm nobody special."

"Did that lady really do all the stuff to you the tabloids said she did?" Mariah presses.

I swallow hard and clear my throat. "I stayed away from the tabloids, so I don't know what they reported. But, Rapture did terrible, demented things. She brainwashed me and sexually assaulted me for years. At times, she acted like she loved me like a second mom. Other times, her relationship with me was far more twisted."

"But you seem so normal now. How did you get to this place?"

"Normal is a relative thing. My friends can tell you I'm not so normal. I can't simply go to the movies or grab a bite to eat. See all these lamps in my office? They're here because I have to be able to control the amount of light in here. I can't trust the overhead lights. I know it doesn't make sense because my boss, Tristan, would never torture me by leaving me in the dark, but I can't risk it. If I don't have control over the light, I can't breathe."

"Oh my gosh! You too?" Mariah exclaims. "I thought it was just me. Pauline and Detective Erickson have me at this super-duper safe place where I'm not supposed to tell people where I stay. It has locks out the wazoo on the windows and doors and there are even cameras around to keep me safe. Despite those precautions, I had to go buy a bunch of nightlights at the discount store. Pauline was worried about me not sleeping. She came up with a brilliant idea."

When I glance up at Pauline, she has tears in her eyes. "I'm not surprised, she's pretty smart."

"She bought me one of those baby toys that lights up and plays lullabies. She thought it might offend me, but the silly toy makes me feel better. When I am feeling stronger, I might ask my mom if I had one when I was little."

"I bet you did," I reply. "I know when I was held captive, one of the strange things I remembered were the layouts of the model train sets my dad and I used to create when I was little. That's the thing I used to focus on when I wanted to separate myself from what was really going on. The memories kept me sane when everything around me was evil."

Mariah wipes tears from her eyes with the heels of her hands. "You seem to be someone who will tell me the truth. Can you answer a question for me?"

"I can try. It depends on what you ask," I hedge.

"I really need to know the answer to this from someone who's been through it. Please don't tell me the answer you think I want to hear. Tell me what I *need* to hear. Tell me the truth even if it's hard and ugly and awful," Mariah pleads.

I get up from my computer chair and walk over to the retro vinyl chair Mariah is sitting in. I squat down in front of her and look her directly in the eyes. "One survivor to another, I won't ever lie to you. But you need to know everyone's experience is different. No one's journey is exactly the same. Even if we were both sexually assaulted, or both mentally abused, or plied with drugs, our backgrounds, psychological makeup and personalities are different. How I cope may be different from how you will. There is no right or wrong way to get through this — some are just healthier than others. For example, I don't recommend drug and alcohol abuse. It only masks the pain that's still there. So, with that caveat, I'll answer your questions as honestly as I can."

"Do the awful memories ever go away? Will I relive them every second of every day forever?" Mariah whispers as tears flow down her face. "I'll be honest with you, if this is what I have to live like for the rest of my life, I don't know if I want to live. All I can hear is the terrible things all those men said about my body. I can't even stand to take a shower and wash my hair. It's part of the reason I cut it all off. I didn't want to take the extra time to wash it and condition it. When it's short, I can wash it in the bathroom sink. I don't even have to get naked."

"The brutally honest answer is the ugly pictures and sounds will always be there. They never truly get erased."

Mariah starts to sob — the kind of sobs which are

silent but cause your whole body to shake. I touch her shoulder to get her attention.

"But, that's not the whole story. It's just the beginning. It's funny, I have a story very similar to yours. My rapist liked my hair long and wavy. If it didn't have enough natural curl to it, she would curl it with a curling iron. She attached weird supernatural mythology to my hair. She believed in her twisted mind that keeping it longer would prevent us from getting caught. So she never let me get my hair cut. I don't know if it was a fetish of hers, or if she was just weird, but the first thing I did when my brother rescued me was shave it all off. For a couple years after I was rescued, I kept it so short I didn't even need to comb it. I couldn't stand the thought of having hair. I didn't want anything which resembled my life as a captive."

"That's how I feel — but I don't fit into my old life either. It's like I don't fit anywhere now. I'm not the person I was before, but I don't want to be the person I was tricked into becoming."

"You don't have to be that person. Those memories, even though they won't completely go away — they will fade. You need to get some counseling. I know that sounds like the last thing you want to do right now. I didn't want to talk about my ordeal either. I just wanted to put it behind me and never think about it again. As hard as I tried, I couldn't get past it until I worked through it with a counselor and a trainer at the gym. I had a lot of pent-up rage. Learning to kickbox helped me channel my rage in a healthy way, instead of turning it inward. Eventually, the horrible slideshow and soundtrack in my head faded. Most of the time, I don't think about those days much anymore until I encounter a trigger."

"But you help find rapists and kidnappers, don't you face triggers every day?" Mariah asks.

"I do. Sometimes, the stories hit close to home. But there's a difference, now I'm the one who has the power. I've discovered by helping other people, I've gained back my self-esteem and autonomy I'd lost for so many years. My kidnapper no longer controls the story of my life. I am in control of how this story plays out. If I want to use my knowledge to catch other bad guys, she can't stop me. It is the most empowering feeling on the planet. It changed me from a victim of a kidnapping to a warrior against crime."

Mariah flashes me a tearful grin. "I want to be a warrior too. No stupid college wanna-be with more good looks than brains is gonna take me down. Let's stop him and all of his scum-ball friends in their tracks."

Chapter Ten

Pauline

I KNEW I HAD the world's best boyfriend, but until today, I didn't really grasp what he's been through. I don't even know if I have the right to call Tobias Payne my boyfriend. We've been out twice. Actually, we don't even go out, but we've intensely hung out together on date substitutions twice and we've gone out for coffee a couple times. Whether or not Toby believes I'm his girlfriend, I consider him my boyfriend. I have absolutely no interest in dating anyone else. A lot of guys I know think they are hot because they dress nice or have cool cars, but I've never met anyone like Toby. The rest of that stuff pales in comparison to what really matters.

Mariah sips on her Frappuccino as we wait at a nearby coffee shop for Cody to arrive. "I know Toby said he didn't want to come. But I think we should take him a sandwich or something. The poor man seemed like he was about to faint from hunger. I've never heard anyone's stomach growl so much."

"That's a great idea. What did you think of Toby?" I ask casually.

"I was surprised. Most guys don't like to talk about

stuff like that. I expected him to give me a line of crap. You know — blow me off and tell me everything is gonna be fine."

"Is that what you wanted him to say?"

Mariah shrugs. "I don't know. Maybe. Sometimes I want somebody to tell me they can wave a magic wand and all this will be over and I can go back to being the person I was before I ever met Heath."

"I can relate a little to what you're saying. When my dad was shot, everything in our lives changed. It was like he became a different person and for a while, things were very scary at my house. I used to pray for time to travel backward so we could relive the day he was shot and do things differently so he would never go on the call."

"But you couldn't do that, could you?"

I shake my head. "No, sadly, we couldn't, and my dad had to get used to being paralyzed on one side."

"Paralyzed is a good way to describe how I've been feeling — but what your friend said really helped. I'm not going to let Heath and all his cronies derail my plans to go to school."

"What are you planning to major in?"

"Originally, I was planning to major in English Lit. and be a college professor. But this experience has been eye-opening. I think I'd like to be a cop like you."

"Mariah, I'm honored — but maybe you should speak to other cops besides me. It's a big career commitment, especially for women."

"Oh, I know. Like Toby says, I have a lot of work to do before I make any big decisions. But it's fun to think about being somebody other than who everyone expects me to be."

My cell phone beeps and I check my messages. "Speaking of other cops, that's Cody. He's waiting in one of the conference rooms at Identity Bank. Are you ready to go talk to him?"

Mariah nods. "I want to see if I can help bust the jerks who did this to me. Because if they did all that to me, who knows how many other girls are out there just like me."

I nod. "Toby reminded me the other day when I stuck my foot in my mouth that it's not only girls. It's boys too."

Mariah crosses her arms in front of herself as she nods her head. "Some of those friends of Heath's were totally strung out. There is no guarantee they wanted to be there anymore than I did."

"Exactly. That's why we're working so hard to stop Heath and all the others like him."

I change the angle of the small video camera as I ask, "You don't mind if we film this, right? It will help us in court if there is a challenge to the way we conducted the questioning. This is especially important since we're not at our police facilities."

"No, go ahead. I'll never forget Heath's face. If you show me his mug shot, the whole world is gonna know. I want to see that jerk pay for what he did to me. I thought I was so special to him. But I realize now he was so good and polished that I'm probably not his first victim. Heck, I'm probably not even his hundredth victim."

Cody shuffles the stacks of pictures in front of him. "It's entirely possible."

"No, think about it. He had like a whole curriculum. It was like Pickpocketing 101. I'm obviously not the only person he's taught to fleece innocent victims. He had a whole lot of criteria for picking lucrative marks. So, if he had a whole system down, there's probably an army of small-town girls from around the nation he tricked into becoming his prostitutes for hire who worked as thieves during the day."

"That's a solid theory. I'm sure there's merit to it. These traffickers get better with practice. It sounds like your trafficker had plenty of practice. I'm going to show you a few pictures. Our persons of interest may or may not be in the array of pictures I will show you. If you can't identify someone that's all right. The people we are looking for may not even be included in this group of pictures."

Mariah frowns. "I'm confused. Why would you bother to show me pictures if the person you want me to find isn't in the pictures?"

"We do it this way to avoid prejudicing you toward a particular candidate over another one," I explain. "It helps eliminate unconscious bias the law enforcement agent might introduce to the process."

"Do you have any questions?" Cody asks Mariah.

"Will something bad happen to me if I don't recognize anyone?"

Cody narrows his eyes. "Do you plan to be truthful?"

Mariah nods. "Of course! I want these creeps caught."

"Then you don't have anything to worry about. Like

I said, you may not recognize anyone in the pictures and that's fine."

I hand Mariah a felt tip pen. "If you see someone you recognize, circle the picture and sign it. Take your time, we're in no hurry."

"Each picture has a number in the lower left-hand corner. I will show them to you one at a time. When I'm finished, you can compare them all. If you want me to stop, you can just say, 'Stop'."

I can see Mariah's breathing quicken as Cody holds up the first picture. After studying it for a few seconds, Mariah shakes her head. "That's not him."

"Okay, what about this one?" Cody asks as he holds up the second picture.

Mariah immediately shakes her head. "No, that's definitely not him."

"Okay, moving on to the next one."

Mariah bites her lip as she studies the third picture. "I went to high school with a guy who looks like this picture, but he is not someone I know from this case."

When Cody holds up the fourth picture, Mariah turns pale. She sways a little in her chair. Wordlessly, she points to the picture and her eyes tear up.

"Mariah? Who is this?" I press.

Mariah grabs a tissue from the box on the table and blows her nose. After she takes a drink of water, she haltingly answers my question. "I don't know for sure. Heath always referred to him as his brother. But I don't know if he meant like literally or not. His nickname for him was The Grouch."

"Did Heath hang out with The Grouch a lot?"

Mariah shrugs. "I always figured Heath got his drugs from The Grouch. They were always talking about money. The Grouch was the one who talked Heath into moving from pickpocketing to licks."

"Licks?" I interrupt to clarify. "Do you mean breaking and entering?"

Mariah nods. "He told him there was more money in robbing people's houses when they weren't at home. They would check the paper and see who was having an estate sale. They figured those houses would have more stuff."

"I have a tough question now. Do you remember if The Grouch was one of the people who sexually assaulted you?"

Mariah blinks away tears. "He was. He was one of the first after Heath. I thought it was weird because I believed The Grouch was Heath's brother which gave me a whole other level of the creeps. I tried to resist, but Heath just beat the snot out of me and I had to sleep with The Grouch anyway."

"Did Heath ever tell you where his so-called brother lived?"

"No, but I wasn't always with it. Heath kept me pretty drugged up."

"Okay, now, I'll move to another stack of pictures. As before, the person we're searching for may or may not be in the stack of pictures."

Mariah's eyes widen when she sees a woman.

"I don't know if I'll be able to identify any of the girls. Whenever he had women over, he made sure I was really drunk or high. I apologize."

"We understand. Just do your best," I encourage.

When Cody shows Mariah the first picture, she shakes her head and wipes away tears. "I'm sorry. Everything is so fuzzy."

"What about this picture?" Cody says as he hands Mariah a picture.

Mariah drops the photo on the conference table. "I don't know her name. But Heath had this woman in his phone. The name in his phone was Fi Fi. I thought it was funny because the name sounded like it should belong to an old lady's poodle or something. I heard him take a call from her once. He thought I was sleeping, but I saw his screen. He referred to her as 'Boss Lady'."

"Do you know anything else about her? Did you ever meet her?" Cody asks.

"I may have, I don't know. I doubt it though. Most of the girls I met were young like me. This woman looks older."

"Do you remember anything about her voice?"

Mariah shakes her head. "No, I couldn't hear her side of the conversation. Heath was super private that way. The only reason I saw him take the phone call at all was because he thought I was asleep. Normally, he didn't take phone calls in front of me."

"Do you remember where you stayed?"

"Heath moved us around from hotel to hotel a lot. I don't know why exactly. I don't know how far we drove. I just know we never made it to Orlando like he promised. We were probably trying to stay away from the police. He liked to go where there were festivals and things to draw tourists. Of course, his choices could have been about where he could score drugs too, for all I know."

"Thank you for taking the time to help us today. Your information has been helpful."

Mariah rolls her eyes. "I don't know how helpful I've been. I didn't know anyone's name or where they're from."

"That's all right. Every little piece of information helps us get closer to the truth. Most of the time, nobody knows everything — a lot of people know a tiny bit and it's up to us to put it all together," I explain. "Eventually, we'll get there. It just takes patience."

I'm not prepared for the sight that greets me when Toby opens his front door. *Umm ... wow! This man should never wear the baggy T-shirts and hoodies he is fond of because they clearly hide the body of a sculpted athlete.* When he sees me staring, he blushes. "Just a second, I wasn't expecting company," he says as he walks over and snags a T-shirt off the back of his couch. I try not to show my disappointment when he puts the T-shirt on and returns to the front door.

I hold up the bag of food from my favorite barbecue place. "I come bearing gifts. Mariah was worried about you. She told me I should feed you. So, I brought you a little of everything."

Toby grins. "I knew there was a reason I liked her. I'm always a fan of food."

"Am I interrupting something?" I ask gesturing toward his casual attire.

Toby looks down at his shorts and T-shirt. "I was just exorcising some ghosts with the heavy bag. Today hasn't been easy."

"Are you okay?"

"Getting there. The workout helped. This will help too," he says as he takes the food from me and sets it out on the kitchen table. I walk over to his cupboards and get dishes and silverware. "You being here will help the most. Thanks for coming," he says gruffly as he reaches out and grabs my arm. He pulls me close for a hug and captures my lips for a thorough kiss. "You are definitely the best part of my day."

"I thought we were coming to see you and Cody for a simple meeting. I had no idea it would turn into such an emotional ordeal. I'm sorry to put you through that."

Toby shrugs. "It happens. Sometimes you don't know what will start an awkward conversation or how the conversation will turn out. I hope what I said was helpful and didn't do more harm than good. Casey should've been the one to talk to her. He has actual psychological training."

"Maybe so. But I think Mariah feels a kinship with you she hasn't yet built with Casey. Perhaps your relationship with her can serve as a bridge. You may not think so, but what you did today was downright heroic. You gave Mariah permission to find herself and fight back."

CHAPTER ELEVEN

TOBY

"Hey, man, I want to thank you," Cody says as he hands me a maple bar and a cup of coffee.

"You're welcome, I guess. What'd I do to deserve this?" I ask as I take a bite.

"When Mariah came to us, she was destroyed. She was willing to cop to things she didn't do simply to avoid going back to her abuser. I hated to see someone so young be totally defeated. Pauline has done a lot to try to get Mariah back on her feet, but she says you're the one who has made the key difference in Mariah's outlook."

"Oh, I don't know if I did much. I was just honest with her about the process I went through."

"You might not think your candor made a difference, but to Mariah it was earth-shattering. You changed her entire worldview."

"I'm glad to help. I'm just sorry we couldn't catch these creeps before they hurt her."

"Thanks to your help, Mariah could give us valuable information we can use to track our suspects."

"Speaking of tracking, do we have any information

on Oscar Brennan?"

"No, surprisingly, most of Felena's contact has been with her soon-to-be ex-husband."

"Those calls are recorded, right?"

"They are," Dylan confirms.

Pauline rushes into the conference room. "Sorry I'm late. I was working on another B & E. I was waiting to see if it might be related to our case."

Dylan raises his eyebrow. "Well, is it?"

Pauline sits down in the chair and throws her files on the table. "Unfortunately not, this was just a spoiled high school kid who was mad at his dad for taking his car keys after he was busted for driving under the influence."

"Charming," I remark. "My dad would've done a lot more than take my car keys away."

"I met with the father," Pauline responds with a smirk. "It's fair to say this guy's punishment radically escalated. He'll be lucky if his dad doesn't escort him into class wearing a pink and purple polka-dotted bikini and sit in the front row with him for the rest of the school year. Dad is not happy."

"Would've been nice to have a lead in our case though," I remark.

"It's funny you should mention that. I think I found one."

Dylan and Cody say in unison, "Why didn't you say anything?"

"Because I finally figured it out on the way here," Pauline replies with a defensive shrug.

"What did you figure out?" I ask with an encouraging

smile.

"Well, you know how we wondered whether Esther Brennan had a stroke after Reginald passed away because she was talking gibberish on the phone?"

"Yeah, the guards reported that none of her conversations made any sense," Cody responds.

Pauline nods enthusiastically. "That's because they were never meant to make sense to us. She was talking in code. When it appeared like she was giving instructions for Reginald's memorial service, she was actually telling Oscar how to continue the business."

"And Oscar was relaying the information to Felena who in turn was telling Bex Michaels?" I surmise.

"That's twisted and brilliant. How in the world did you figure it out?" Cody asks as he salutes her.

Pauline blushes as she explains. "I got to thinking about Toby's explanation about how coding works and how he looks for patterns when he's looking for glitches. Something struck me about Esther's abrupt change in language after Reginald died. I looked at her medical records and there was no health reason why she would be speaking oddly. When I was in junior high school, my friends and I came up with this coded language so we could talk to each other without other girls knowing what we were saying. We thought it made us seem cool. We probably sounded idiotic to everyone else — but, we were convinced we were all that."

"Doesn't everyone think everybody else is idiotic in junior high school? I thought it was a rite of passage," I tease.

Pauline wrinkles her nose at me. "Probably so. Anyway, those extra nonsensical words were bugging me, so I wrote them down. It turns out they weren't so nonsensical after all. Esther was conveying messages to Oscar. She was giving him passwords and websites."

"Which Oscar shared with his new 'girlfriend' and she passed on to her sicko husband," I guess, completing her thought.

"Bingo!" Pauline replies. "Give the man a gold star. What we don't know is if Oscar is working with Bex Michaels intentionally or if Felena Hopner is double-crossing Oscar and working with the competition."

I chuckle as I pause to drink my coffee. "Nobody said there was honor among sociopaths. It will be interesting to see them destroy each other."

"Mariah wanted me to show this to you," Pauline says as she pushes a picture toward my side of the table as we set up a new 3D puzzle.

"Natalie took these pictures of her mom cooking with Mariah. Apparently, this is the first batch of croissants Mariah made by herself. She's pretty proud of them."

I grin. "She should be! Croissants are not like making biscuits from a can."

"Mariah wanted me to let you know she's taking lots of baby steps. She is getting her high school diploma through a program offered by Uncommon Paths. She and Savannah have tightly bonded over their shared experiences. Things are going really well. She told me to tell you thank you for giving her a 'kick in the pants'."

"Is that what I did? I don't know. I wonder if I was too honest about how hard the road would be in the future?"

Pauline shakes her head. "I can't speak for Mariah but I know when we were dealing with the aftermath of my father's shooting if a doctor or a therapist tried to sugarcoat things and tell us everything was going to be fine when it was obvious they weren't, I immediately distrusted them and dismissed everything they had to say. If a nurse, doctor or therapist told me the gritty, honest truth — even if it was hard, my respect for them went up several notches. I bet it was the same way with Mariah. She was probably tired of people lying to her."

"Some truths are too painful to hear. I hope I didn't cross the line."

Pauline sets the puzzle piece in her hand down and walks over to my side of the table. She pulls me up to a standing position and wraps her arms around my neck as she says, "Relax. If she wasn't looking for information, she would've never asked you for your input. She needed your help, and you gave it to her. She was stuck, and you gave her the push she needed. It was help she wasn't ready to get from Casey quite yet. She needed to understand the truth from you. Sometimes we need to hear things from different perspectives to understand. I think that's where she was at."

"I know. I just wish she didn't need to know that. My story is so dark and ugly. No one should need to hear the details of what I went through to be able to navigate their own story. I guess that's what bothers me about the whole situation."

"I understand. Neither one of us can undo what's happened to her. The best we can do is help her navigate through the best way we can. You gave her invaluable tools to regain her footing and get the help she needs. I'm so proud of you. I know it couldn't have been easy." Pauline stands on her tiptoes and pulls my lips toward hers and kisses me gently.

I deepen the kiss and hug her close, drawing strength from her presence.

"Mmm, I could get used to that," Pauline says with a contented sigh as she pulls away and gathers her hair back into a ponytail. "Are you sure you want to spend our time together doing a puzzle? I can think of more exciting things to do."

With a grin, I pull the hair tie out of her silken tresses. Her hair falls like a modern version of Rapunzel. "Oh, you can, huh? I kind of like the puzz —"

Just then the unmistakable squeal of brakes being applied interrupts the strains of Sam Smith playing softly in the background. An instant later horrific sounds of crunching metal echoes through the quiet house and the lights suddenly dim plunging us into darkness.

I am frozen, unable to move or process thought in the suffocating darkness. My heart pounds as I fight to keep my mind from racing back to years I'd rather forget. Through my mental fog, I hear Pauline barking my address to someone on her cell phone. From the snippets of conversation I'm picking up, I presume it's someone from dispatch. Much to my horror, my teeth start to chatter. Pauline hangs up her phone and activates her flashlight. She reaches into my pocket and removes my cell phone and turns on my flashlight as well. She puts her arm around my waist and leads me toward the front door. Without a moment of hesitation, she grabs her service weapon and holster and buckles it around her waist before she puts on her jacket. She takes a sweatshirt off the hook and steers us out the door.

"W-What are we doing?" I stammer.

"The house isn't a healthy environment for you right now," she explains as she puts me into her SUV, puts her key in the ignition, and turns on the dome light.

As the light fills the vehicle, I struggle to breathe and relax my muscles. Vaguely I hear her make another phone call. She pokes her head in the SUV. "How are you doing? Someone will be here in a second to hang out with you — but I have to go. I need to make sure everyone is okay at the accident scene. But I don't want to leave you if you're not okay."

I clear my throat and point to the dome light. "I'll survive. I've survived much worse. Go. I'm fine. I've got light now."

As she turns to leave, I kick myself as coherent thought starts to return. "Are you gonna be safe?"

"Yeah, I'll be fine. Backup will be here any second. I need to do a preliminary assessment and see if there's anything I need to do right now. I'll be back."

Pauline reaches back and gives my shoulder a squeeze through the window before she takes off running.

As I watch her disappear into the darkness, my heart pounds. I turn the radio up to distract me from the pitch-black night. "Why do I have to be such a wuss about this? Why can't I be heroic like Jameson?" I ask the universe, never expecting an answer.

My heart jumps in my throat when someone opens the other side of the SUV and gets in. "I guess it depends on your perspective, son. My daughter happens to think you are the very definition of heroic," Desmond

Lawrence replies as if I addressed him.

"Sir, I was anything but a hero. When the lights went out, my post-traumatic stress disorder hit so hard I couldn't move. If your daughter had been in danger, it would've been impossible for me to save her. I couldn't even save myself."

"Yeah, PTSD is a heckuva thing, isn't it? It's part of the reason I wasn't cleared for a desk job after I was shot. Every time somebody reached their hand out to shake mine, I swore up and down I saw a gun, even though nobody was out to hurt me. I felt crazier than a loon. To this day, if somebody moves quickly, I still flinch and duck. Let me tell you, it makes going out in public a little awkward."

"I wasn't able to protect Pauline from potential danger. If something would've happened to her, it would've been all my fault," I admit.

Des pats my shoulder. "In case you haven't noticed, my daughter can protect herself and you perfectly fine. In fact, she considers it her responsibility to take care of both of us."

"Well, maybe not since she contacted you to babysit me."

"Nonsense, my little girl is one of the most sensitive creatures on the whole planet. She knew you'd need a friend who would understand what you're going through tonight. I hated the lessons I learned from being shot — but maybe, just maybe, they'll be of value now. I think Pauline meant for us to get through this together. I know it meant the world to me as a police officer to know my family was safe and happy at home while I was working hard to save the world. Let's give Pauline some of that peace of mind."

"That's true, your daughter makes me very happy. Still, because I am who I am, I'll feel a lot safer once power is restored to my house. I'm sorry, I can't pretend otherwise."

Desmond grins at me. "Pauline once told me I could expect nothing but honesty from you. I appreciate that quality in a person. The reason my daughter wanted me to come here tonight was to invite you back to our house until your power is restored. Christie cooked a delightful dinner tonight. I know that there are leftovers with your name on them. You might as well make yourself comfortable. If I know anything about how these calls go, Pauline will be here for a while."

"I appreciate the offer. I wish I had brought my computer with me so I could get some work done on the case."

"If you're anything like me, you'll be thinking about it anyway. So, just take some downtime and enjoy a good meal. The case will still be there when your power comes back on."

Chapter Twelve

Pauline

I CRINGE WHEN MY parents' front door squeaks as I close
it behind me. Wearily, I remove my service weapon and
holster and place them in the gun safe my dad used for
years. I take my jacket off and stretch out my shoulders
and neck. Fortunately, the accident wasn't severe. No one
was fatally injured. It seems the driver experienced the
worst of it with just a fractured wrist. However, he took
out a transformer and plunged several neighborhoods
into darkness. So, I ended up directing traffic in a Florida
monsoon. I haven't done that since my early days as a cop.
I can't say I miss it much.

I walk quietly back to my bedroom and grab my
favorite sweats and a sweatshirt before I turn the shower
on. I hope the sound of running water doesn't wake my
dad. He doesn't sleep well these days, but I have to warm
up. Even the coat I borrowed from the fire department
didn't keep me dry at the accident scene and I feel frozen
to the bone. When I'm finished with my shower, I dry my
hair as efficiently as I can with a towel and braid it. I dress
in my sweats and sweatshirt, pulling the hood up over my
wet hair and I put on my favorite fuzzy slippers which

resemble Cookie Monster.

Yawning, I head down to the kitchen to see what I can find to eat. I smile when I see a plate filled with homemade macaroni and cheese, green beans and creamed corn covered with cling wrap. My stomach growls as I pop it in the microwave. Many people razz me for still living with my parents at my age. But after the kind of day I've had, these are the type of perks which keep me satisfied with my living arrangements. It's not so bad. I have my own private room and bathroom. I'm so busy at my job, I hardly notice anyway. It seems to work for everyone, so I'm in no hurry to move.

Grabbing a couple oven mitts from the drawer, I take the plate out of the microwave and carry it to the kitchen table. I jump when I hear someone cough in the living room. Cautiously, I go investigate. My eyes widen when I see Toby sacked out in my dad's favorite La-Z-Boy. He is covered by my mom's favorite quilt and illuminated by the light she uses to do her cross-stitch.

When I approach, Toby opens his eyes. At first, he appears dazed and confused. But when I hand him his glasses, he smiles. "Is everyone okay?"

I nod. "No one was seriously hurt in the accident. Traffic was a little gnarly without lights for a while, but even those came on eventually. I figured my dad would take you home."

"Your dad had such a great time telling me war stories, he got a little tuckered out. He was on the verge of falling asleep before the power came back on. I told your mom I didn't mind staying here."

"In this weather it was probably a safer choice anyway. There might be power lines down between my house and yours. You want something to eat? My mom dished up more than I need."

Toby shrugs. "I won't turn it down. It was delicious."

I walk back to the kitchen and grab a plate and divide my dinner between the two plates and hand Toby an extra fork. "Are you feeling better since the lights are back on? I'm sorry I had to bail on our date."

Toby flinches. "I'm fine now. But… will *you* be okay? The crap you saw tonight? That kind of stuff happens to me all the time. I can be fine one minute and in a completely different headspace the next with absolutely no warning. Today's episode was mild. Sometimes I can be messed up for weeks at a time. You have enough to deal with. I'm not sure you need my craziness too."

"Do you hear me complaining?" I pause to take a few bites of my dinner. "Listen, everybody's got something. Nobody in a relationship is perfect — except on TV or in the movies. Everybody has emotional scars or physical or mental differences. That's life. If we were all the same, it would be exceptionally boring. I don't do boring very well, in case you haven't noticed."

Toby puts his hand over mine to get my attention. "Pauline, I'm messed up. This is more than just a little personality quirk. Rapture did serious damage. She changed me in ways which will have profound effects on us forever. I just want to make sure you get that."

I take a sip of my Pepsi as I try to choose my words carefully. It's late and I'm exhausted. I already have a tendency to stick my foot in my mouth whenever I'm around Toby. I don't want to make an awkward conversation even worse by saying something profoundly stupid I don't even mean.

"Toby, I like you a lot. I have ever since we worked together on the case of the missing teens a couple years ago. Being in the same room with you makes my heart race a little faster and the words tumble out of my mouth in random order sometimes. Occasionally, I've said epically stupid stuff in front of you. I've apologized to you more than I've apologized to anyone — ever. So, I'll probably get things wrong between us because I can't possibly understand everything you've ever been through because I can't know. I haven't been in your shoes. I'm willing to try to understand and to support you. I can go to counseling and learn about post-traumatic stress disorder or relationship counseling for partners of sexual assault victims. Just tell me what I need to do."

Toby rakes his hand through his hair in frustration. "You're the first person I've let close enough to see this side of me. I don't know if this is even the kind of thing you can learn to help with. I kinda think I have to fight my demons on my own."

I stand up and walk around the table until I'm standing behind Toby. "People often accuse me of being a little too optimistic, but I'm choosing to look on the bright side of your statement." I tip his head back and kiss him on the lips.

Toby looks up at me incredulously. "There's a bright side to our conversation? I just told you I'm royally messed up!"

"Uh-huh, but you know what else you told me? You said I matter to you and I'm your first serious girlfriend. To a woman like me that means the world. Whatever it takes, I'm willing to fight for us."

"I appreciate your enthusiasm, but you need to understand, I'm not a case you have to solve. There is more to me than my past and I'm not a series of puzzle pieces for you to put together and fix. There will be good days and bad, but I'll never be the person I would have been if the kidnapping and rape hadn't happened. What happened to me will impact me *and us* for the rest of my life."

The waiter pours me another glass of ice water with a twist of lemon, but I can't miss the look of sympathy in his eyes before he walks away. Under the best of circumstances, I get antsy at these law enforcement recognition dinners. These are not definitely ideal circumstances.

I close my eyes and lean my head against the wall as I fight back tears. I open them when I hear someone slide into the seat next to me. "You okay?" Lauren, Dylan Palmer's fiancé, asks as she studies me. "Is your blood sugar crashing? You want me to sneak back into the kitchen and grab you a bite to eat? It's taking them way too long to get the food out. I'm about ready to throw on a chef's jacket and go help them."

I shake my head. "No, I'm fine. These fancy dinners are always hard for me anyway. I don't like to dress up and sit still. I ate a granola bar before I came. I'm just having a tough day."

"Anything I can help with?"

I roll my shoulder. "I don't know. I'm having problems with Toby. I thought we had talked through them … but maybe not. He was supposed to be here a long time ago." I pick up my phone and check the time for what seems like the thousandth time. "He's still not here and he hasn't sent a text or anything. Maybe things are worse between us than I thought."

Lauren nods. "Yeah, I know all about relationship issues. Dylan and I have had a few. New courtships can be especially challenging."

"I'm so confused. I thought I was being helpful and supportive. Unfortunately, Toby took it all wrong. Now, he thinks I'm trying to solve all his problems like he's one of my cases."

Lauren takes a drink of her sweet tea. After she puts it down, she bites her bottom lip and then speaks, "Keep in mind I'm about to marry a guy who is every bit as intense as you are, if not more. So, I don't mean this question as a putdown of any sort — but are you? I know sometimes Dylan has a hard time leaving his job at work."

My first instinct is to push back against her question. But then I draw in a deep breath and let it out. "Geez, I don't know! I like to solve problems. It's what makes me good at my job."

Lauren nods. "Exactly. Dylan says you are one of the most talented young detectives he's ever worked with. But Toby's not your job, is he?"

Mutely, I shake my head.

"To tell you the truth, I have such a collection of problems, I wondered if I would ever find anyone to spend my life with. Between my family history and my panic attacks, I'm a difficult person to love. But Dylan and I found things work better between us if we focus on what we're great at instead of what makes us feel weak."

"Does that mean you don't let Dylan help you?"

"No, sometimes, I still need his help to get me out of a particularly bad panic attack or to help prepare me to make a presentation in front of a bunch of people. But, it's no longer Dylan's responsibility to fix me. With his help, I've developed tools to advocate for myself.

Because of Dylan, I have Sara Lee and I'm in therapy to cope with my anxiety. I would have never taken those steps without his encouragement."

"Aren't those just semantics though? Dylan is still helping you through the tough times — like I offered to do for Toby."

"I know it sounds the same, but it's not. Dylan gave me back my power. He is not in charge of fixing things any more. Although being with him makes me very happy, he's not in charge of my happiness. I am. For the first time in my life, I feel empowered. That shift in the balance of power made it possible for me to believe in myself and the power of love."

"Wow! You should put that in your wedding vows. That's deep stuff there," I remark as I dab away tears.

Lauren smiles. "Already working on it. I don't know Toby well, I've only met him a couple of times, but he may need you to give him the power to find his own definition of happiness and what it means to include you in his life."

Tears flow down my face. "I know you'll soon be the wife of my training partner, but do you suppose it would be against the rules for you to be my BFF?"

Lauren puts her arm around my shoulders and gives me a hug. "I don't really care. Dylan knows I don't follow the rules so closely."

I grin through my tears. "Well, he totally knows that about me. So the two of us together could be unbelievably dangerous."

"Better get back to my table. Dylan's parents and sister will be here soon. They are bursting with pride to see him get honored by the governor for his work on the

Cold Case Squadron. I know he feels like he doesn't deserve any recognition since he didn't find my sister alive, but he has helped so many other families during his career he should get this recognition. I am so proud of him."

"You should be. He's been a wonderful mentor. I hope someday I'm as good a cop as he is. More importantly, I hope I turn out to be half as good a human being as Dylan is."

"From everything I have heard, you're well on your way. Try not to worry. I'm sure things with Toby aren't as bad as they seem."

The waiter smiles at me when he delivers my Chicken Cordon Bleu and asparagus. Just as he's about to clear away Toby's place setting, Toby enters the ballroom. His pants leg is covered in mud and his jacket sleeve is torn. I gasp and stand up to greet him. "Oh my gosh! Are you okay?"

He shrugs. "I've had better days." He tosses his phone on the table, showing me the shattered face.

"What happened?" I demand as I run my hands across his body, feeling for broken bones. He winces when I reach his left shoulder.

"I had a medical appointment, and the doctor ran late — but I was on my way here when I saw this older gentleman trying to change his tire on the side of the freeway. So, I pulled over to help him. That's what you do when you're a Payne. I may not be a soldier like my brother, but I know the right thing to do."

"Like there was ever any doubt."

"So, Javier and I were changing his tire. Things were going as well as could be expected, I suppose. My jack didn't fit his car, so we had to use his cheap jack and one of the lug nuts was rusted on because it was an ancient car. I almost had the nut off when a stupid looky-loo hit the car in front of him."

I swallow hard, remembering my days on traffic detail. "Oh no!"

"'Oh no' is a bit of an understatement. The car jack gave way, and I tweaked my shoulder, Javier stepped on my phone, and the car that was hit slammed into my car which was parked on the side of the road as if it was a bumper car."

Resisting the urge to hug Toby tightly, I restrain myself. A million questions bounce around in my brain. I fight the urge to fall into cop mode and start fixing things. That's not what I'm here for. Tonight, I'm just Toby's girlfriend. I struggle to keep my voice casual. "I am so sorry. What do you need from me?"

"I'm freezing and starving. It was wet and muddy out there and I haven't eaten since breakfast."

I push my dinner plate toward him. "I don't have any coffee, but I'll get you some."

The waiter, who apparently had been eavesdropping throughout the whole conversation, steps forward. "No need to do that ma'am. I can get him his choice of roast beef or chicken." The waiter turns to Toby. "Which would you prefer, sir?"

"Roast beef, I guess."

"Cream and sugar in your coffee?"

Toby wearily nods.

"Can I catch a ride home with you? I don't want to ride the bus. My car is out of commission at the moment. I hope the speeches don't last too long. I want to go home."

I catch the waiter's eye and he nods.

"No problem. I was never big on speeches. The way I know Cody, he'll make a video of every second of Dylan's speech anyway. We can leave right now if you want. Do you need to go to the ER and get your shoulder checked out?"

Toby shivers dramatically. "Nah, I avoid the doctor whenever possible. I'll just take a shower and a few anti-inflammatories. I'll ice it tonight. If it's not better in a couple days, I might get it checked out."

"Promise me you won't be a tough guy on this one. Shoulders can be gnarly if you have an untreated injury. If it still bothers you after a few days, make sure you tell somebody, okay?"

Toby raises an eyebrow. "Yes, Mama," he teases.

I blush. "So sue me for caring. One of my friends from the police academy had to wash out because she tore her rotator cuff and didn't take care of it."

"I was just kidding. Thanks for watching out for me. It's been a massively rough day. Sometimes, I'm not as funny as I think I am."

"When you didn't show up for dinner, I was afraid you were still mad at me," I admit.

"Pauline, I wasn't ever mad at you. That was never what our conversation was about. I was angry that a person I thought I buried long ago in my past still haunts my future. I'm still trying to figure out how to deal with all the garbage she left behind."

"In case it's not clear to you, there is a lot more to you than the garbage she left behind. If you don't believe me, ask Javier. You sacrificed your body, your car and your phone to help him change his tire. Not very many people would volunteer. I'm proud to call you my boyfriend."

Toby closes his eyes for a second. When he reopens them, a bit of the pain has cleared away. "Thanks, I needed to hear that."

The waiter returns with three large to-go boxes. "I boxed you guys up a couple of nice dinners. I included several kinds of dessert. Go home and pamper yourself. You deserve it. My grandpa's name is Gustav, but it could've been Javier. Thank you for being somebody's hero tonight. There is too much hate in the world."

"Thanks. I was only doing what any decent human being would have done."

"That's the problem. There aren't enough people like you left in the world."

I glance down at the three large boxes of food and the huge to-go cup of coffee. "All evidence to the contrary. Thank you for taking such good care of us tonight. Have a good evening. I'm going to go bandage up my hero and make sure he has medicine to kill his pain."

CHAPTER THIRTEEN

TOBY

THE CLOCK ON THE wall seems to tick as loud as a cannon as we wait for the task force meeting to begin. Pauline shoots me worried looks as she arranges the boxes of fancy donuts in the middle of the table. I don't blame her. Anyone else in my shoes would be ecstatic over the recent developments in my life. Pauline is thoroughly confused and worried sick.

Join the club, babe. So am I. Sometimes, it sucks to be me.

Tristan comes into the conference room grinning from ear to ear. "The blue work okay for you? I considered red, but I figure it was a little flashy for your personality. The blue color is called Blue Jeans. When I found out, I knew it was the perfect match for you."

I adjust myself in my seat and try not to jostle my shoulder as I square myself up with my boss. "You sure you want to talk about this here?"

Tristan looks around the table at Cody and Dylan. "Sure, everyone here is your friend … or more." He winks at Pauline. "Everyone is my friend too, or at least I like to think so."

"Okay ... but this conversation might not go the way you were expecting."

Tristan chuckles. "That happens to me more often than you might expect."

"You want to tell me why I found a brand-new truck parked in my driveway?"

"Cause some knucklehead smashed your car?" replies Tristan with a look of pure innocence.

I roll my eyes. "I'm aware. I'm still waiting for my insurance agent to return my phone call so I can turn in my paperwork."

"So, my timing was perfect," Tristan announces in a self-congratulatory tone.

"No, no it wasn't. I didn't earn that truck. I work for you and you pay me well for what I do. But I did nothing to deserve a new truck. I don't accept gifts from people. Not like this."

Tristan appears shell-shocked. "Umm, I'm sorry. I didn't mean to offend you. I was only trying to be helpful."

"Oh, I know. I didn't mean to suggest you were trying to be offensive. Life has taught me a few profoundly painful lessons. I learned a long time ago that if it seems too good to be true, it probably is. Let's face it, most people just aren't that nice. I had a person bribe me with all sorts of expensive gifts. In the beginning, Rapture provided everything I ever wished for in our so-called friendship. It's how she tricked me into trusting her. I swore I'd never put myself in that kind of position again. So, these days, I don't accept presents I don't earn — even from friends ... or well-meaning bosses."

Tristan leans back in his chair and scrubs his hand down his face. "Wow! That sure puts a different spin on things, doesn't it? This has been an eye-opening conversation. I was merely trying to make your life easier and reward you for being a superb example of the attitude of giving I like to see at Identity Bank. I deeply respect employees who go above and beyond to help total strangers simply because it's the right thing to do. I never dreamed my gift would dredge up painful memories for you. I apologize."

"It's okay. There is no way you could've predicted my level of weirdness. You probably could've given the truck to ten thousand employees and they would've been thrilled to get it. You just had the bad fortune to hire me with my issues. Sorry to make it so complicated."

"Hmm, interesting point. The truck is yours. It's fully paid for. If you don't want it, what do you want to do with it?"

Tristan's question takes me off guard. I figured he would just take the truck back to the dealership or something. Who has sixty grand lying around? Oh right. Tristan does. It's like pocket change to him. "You like working with Habitat for Humanity. Maybe they need it."

"Possibly. I give them lots of money and time already, though. What about a smaller cause?"

"What about Zoe's work with service dogs. You know, the Critter Coach?" I suggest.

"Oh my gosh!" Pauline interjects. "I saw a dog she trained the other night. Sara Lee was the most precious thing. Lauren was telling me all about how Sara Lee gave her a sense of independence she'd never had before. I think that's an excellent idea!"

I sigh. "There's only one problem. Phoenix and Zoe are based in Oregon — just like me. A truck in Florida doesn't do them much good."

Dylan shakes his head. "I've gotten so used to working with you I forget you're a transplanted Oregonian now."

Pauline looks glum. "You're not the only one who has amnesia about that topic."

Tristan clears his throat. "This might be an excellent time to remind you I'm an extremely benevolent boss. If it would be more beneficial for you to work for Identity Bank in Florida, I have no objection. If Zoe and Phoenix need a truck, just say the word."

My jaw goes slack. "You would pay to have the truck shipped all the way to Oregon just to give it away?"

Tristan shakes his head. "No, I'd probably have them choose one to meet their needs. You can give yours away a little closer to Florida."

"Okay, I'll give it to Mitch at Hope's Haven. He could probably use it in his work with search and rescue dogs."

"Sounds like a plan. Can you do me a favor, though?"

I shrug.

"Will you use the truck until your insurance company comes through with a replacement rig? Sometimes stuff pops up on the job and I need you to be available when the buses don't run."

"I suppose it wouldn't hurt me to borrow it for a couple weeks until I can get another vehicle. Although honestly, I'm sure I'll get spoiled by all the bells and whistles. You chose a sweet rig."

Tristan grins. "I hate to make you suffer even for a

little while. Hopefully, the insurance company will reward you for being a Good Samaritan and give you a generous payout for your damaged car and you can buy your own dream truck."

I pick up the remote for the projector screen and flip open a file. "Now that you guys know way more than you need to about my personal life, why don't we talk about what this meeting is supposed to be about?"

As soon as the first image appears, Dylan groans. "Not Ignis Fatuus Hex again! I thought we shut his site down when Bex Michaels went to prison."

"I thought so too — but I have an alert on the site just in case. Sure enough, about six days ago, it registered some new activity."

Pauline's brows furrow. "What kind of new activity?"

"He appears to be up to his old tricks. If it's not him, someone pretending to be him is recruiting talent to be in his videos again."

"I'm recruitable. My cover wasn't blown during the last bust. As far as he knows, I was just one of the teens who got arrested and was released back to my parents. If I go back, it will lend credence to my story that I am determined to make it as a country music star," Pauline suggests.

"No!" I blurt reflexively.

Pauline bristles. "What do you mean, no? My cover wasn't blown. I was extremely careful to stay in character. The feds who arrested me didn't even know I was a law enforcement officer until well after the fact. That's part of the reason I got in so much trouble, remember?"

"As I recall, you got called on the carpet because you didn't have backup before you went in on your own. If it hadn't been for the feds having their own operation, no one would've known you had infiltrated Bex Michaels' organization. You could have gotten yourself killed," Cody interjects.

"Okay, *technically* that's correct. But I didn't, and I was able to collect information which led to the recovery of dozens of teenagers. So, it all worked out. I won't make the same mistake again. We can get backup lined up for me in advance. I'm not planning to go in blind this time."

"These are incredibly dangerous sociopathic people — generations of them. I know what it's like to be held by people like this. You shouldn't put yourself in that kind of danger! It's too risky. There has to be another way!"

Pauline whirls around and stares at me with white-hot rage in her eyes. "Are you saying you don't think I'm capable of handling this? Did you miss the part of the discussion where I graduated top of my class at the police academy? By the way, I didn't have them make the physical requirements easier for me because I'm female. I competed stride for stride, push-up for push-up, sit-up for sit-up. I've been rehearsing for the physical requirements at the Academy since I was about ten years old. My dad ran me through those drills as soon as I was big enough to handle the equipment. Do you know I'm more proficient with my weapon than my firearms instructor? I shoot equally well right and left-handed. Not very many people can say that. You know, a lot of people say I got this job because of who my dad is. They automatically assume I benefited from nepotism. Not surprisingly, those people never even bother to look at my grades or my letters of recommendation. I made sure I got letters from people who had never even met my father. I'm used to dealing with people who don't believe in my skills or my qualifications, I just never expected that person to be you."

"Pauline, I didn't mean —"

She picks up her files and heads toward the door. "I'll let you guys discuss the case. Obviously, my input isn't needed."

Before I can say a word, Pauline is out the door. Only Tristan's dedication to quality construction prevents the door from slamming behind her.

For several moments the three of us look around the room in shock. Eventually, I break the silence. "I'm not wrong. What she's asking to do is crazy dangerous and may not even be successful. If it's really Bex Michaels, there's a good chance he may remember her from before. That would make what's already an insanely risky plan exponentially more treacherous."

"But the Rookie is right too. Her role in taking down Bex Michaels and rescuing his victims is often overshadowed by the fact that Captain Schumaker had to reprimand her for not organizing a formal operation and getting backup first. What she did was gutsy and showed razor-sharp instincts. She saved those kids' lives. I hate to say it, but if she would've been a guy, she would have been hailed as the hero of the department. Dylan and I have trained a lot of cops. Pauline is one of the best we've ever worked with."

"This is crazy! She's asking to be kidnapped. I lived that nightmare. What if something goes wrong?"

"We are here to make sure it doesn't," Cody says confidently.

"Think of it this way," Dylan adds. "If it isn't Pauline with a full backup team, he'll target some other starry-eyed teenager with big dreams and no idea what's about to happen to them. Do we really want to be searching for more kids like DeAndre, Isadora and Tallulah?"

"No! If I had my way, people like Bex and Rapture would be eaten alive by mutant scavengers and left to die in the middle of the desert."

Tristan grimaces. "Nice visual, buddy. You know how helping catch kidnappers and pedophiles helps you make sense of your past and gives you strength? I have a sense that fighting evil does the same for your girlfriend. I know it's hard to see her put herself in danger. But, I think it's not a choice for her. I believe it's part of her DNA as much as being computer nerds is part of who we are."

"I feel so helpless. How do we keep her safe?"

"By refining our software program so we can identify every single creep around her. We gotta find a way to get down to the micro-level. If they have ketchup with their hash browns for breakfast, we need to know."

"On it, Boss! Let's bust these guys for good this time. I don't want to lose anyone else — especially not Pauline. I don't know how this happened, but she somehow became the most important person in my world. I can't imagine my life without her in it."

Cody looks at me intently. "Does Pauline know you feel that way?"

I shrug. "I don't know if I've actually said those words out loud."

"You know, when you work in our field, there is no such thing as a routine call. My former partner was almost killed on what should've been a routine, simple no drama call. Don't let words go unsaid between you. The Rookie needs to know how you feel. She needs to know you believe in her and have her back."

I close my eyes and shake my head as I try to clear the ugly slide show of horrors from my past which is suddenly playing on autopilot. "Will I ever stop being terrified for her well-being?"

Cody chuckles softly. "No, sorry I think it's part of the price of being in love. Every time I see Tori facing a crush of photographers after a trial, I still hold my breath. I know I can't wrap her in bubble wrap. But after all the terrible lies and innuendos she faced before, it's still difficult for me to accept that talking to reporters is part of her job as district attorney. Every time I see someone stick a microphone in her face, I want to slam them to the ground for the pain they caused her."

I smirk. "It probably wouldn't be the best strategy to improve the public's perception of the police department."

Cody sighs. "I know. That's why Tori tells me I need to behave. But, sometimes fighting your natural instincts for love is hard."

Chapter Fourteen

Pauline

How can one inbox get filled with so much spam? This is supposed to be my official work account. I shake my head in frustration as I absentmindedly clear out my inbox and drink coffee in the very plush break room at Identity Bank.

Okay, let's just be honest. I'm trying to keep my mind off of the meeting in the other room. I was only trying to make a point. Toby hurt my feelings. I know I screwed up an operation a couple years ago — but a lot of good came out of my mistake. Am I going to spend the rest of my career living down one miscalculation? I'm a good cop, darn it! So, why did I let my mouth run and undermine my own argument? I know I'll hear about this from Cody and Dylan. They can stand in line. I'm already kicking my own butt. I'm just fortunate I screwed up here and not back at headquarters. Captain Schumaker doesn't need any more reasons to be upset with me.

Trying to calm my nerves, I go over to the coffee machine to top off my cup. As I'm doctoring it with cream and sugar, I hear Cody's voice behind me. "You should be okay with coffee, but stay away from the microwave. It's possessed."

"You haven't been here the last couple days. That's a new one," Tristan replies.

"Finally! I was getting tired of peanut butter and jelly sandwiches. Thanks for getting it fixed," Toby adds.

Cody and Dylan walk into the break room and sit at one of the large tables. Dylan is studying my body language carefully. After a while, his prolonged silence is too much and I blurt, "Well, don't keep me in suspense. Did you all figure out how to solve this case without me? Do I go back to writing traffic tickets?"

Tristan smirks, as he makes a gesture for me to sit. "You remind me a lot of my wife. You're smart. But you have a lot of sass." He gives me a pointed look. "Sometimes a little too much if I don't miss my guess."

I blush as I grab my coffee and sit down. "Wouldn't be the first time someone has mentioned something similar."

Cody takes his ever-present notebook out of his pocket. "Rookie, if you're done throwing your snit, we can start planning this operation properly, so you don't die."

"Operation? So I'm in? Seriously?" I ask, unable to keep my cool or hide my excitement.

"Your idea had lots of merit. So, we'll make the case to the captain. However, before we do that, we have to plug all the holes and make sure you're as secure as you would be in your own house."

I sigh. "You guys have met my dad. That's a tall order. I'm not even sure it's possible."

Toby nods. "Desmond is a stickler for detail, that's a

given. You know I have serious reservations about this mission —"

"You can't protect me just because I'm your girl —" I protest abruptly.

"Yes, I have issues, but it's not only because you're my girlfriend. I would have issues with anyone we sent in. Anyone will be a sitting duck. That's why we have to make this operation the safest one we've ever done. Having been a kidnapping victim for years, I think this idea is absolutely insane. But you are a brilliant cop, so I have to put my protective instincts aside and let you do your job. But that won't mean I won't have nightmares every single night until this job is done. Do you understand? It's not because I don't think you're amazing, spectacular and the smartest woman I know. It's because I know what might happen to you if it all goes wrong."

"Okay. Understood. So, let's go use your smarts to make sure nothing goes wrong. I don't want anything to happen to any other victims. I'm in a unique position to stop it and I have the best backup team in the business."

I narrow my eyes as I concentrate on the teenage girl's body movements as she competes on a national singing competition. That's the thing about this job, I can't say it's boring. Captain Schumaker reluctantly gave his approval to Dylan's plan to send me undercover with the understanding I would have extensive backup from both our department and the resources of Identity Bank.

Most of the time, my time is spent demonstrating how mature I am for my age. I'm usually the youngest law enforcement agent in the room and I always have to prove I am a capable, equal partner even though I look fragile and young. On this assignment, the opposite is true. I'm trying to play up my youth and innocence. Although people often comment about how young I look, compared to these teenagers, I don't feel so young. Even though my high school graduation was only a few years ago, compared to these kids, I feel downright ancient.

As I click on another video, my phone rings. "Pauline Lawrence, Detective Division."

I hear a sob followed by, "I saw him! I saw him! I swear, I saw him!"

"Mariah?" I guess. "Where are you? Are you safe?"

"I'm safe. I'm driving to your office."

I hand Mariah a cup of hot coffee and place a blanket around her shoulders. "Are you sure you don't need me to take you to the hospital?" I ask as I watch her struggle to catch her breath as her teeth chatter.

She carefully sets the cup of coffee on the table and wipes away tears with the back of her hand. "I'll be fine," she answers softly. "He just totally freaked me out. I don't know if he knew it was me because I have a new car and the windows are tinted, but I'm sure it was him. I almost passed out."

"Are you okay now? Maybe I should give you a few minutes to settle before I ask you any questions," I respond as I study her closely.

"No! I don't want to wait. I want you to find Heath before he can hurt anyone else."

I swallow hard as the ramifications of what she's asking me to do fly through my head. I am stuck between the proverbial rock and hard place. I've spent months building a rapport with Mariah. I need her to trust in my ability to protect her. Now for reasons I can't fully explain, I have to bow out of the hunt for Heath.

Plastering a reassuring smile on my face, I forge ahead. "I understand. We want to work with you to catch him. What can you tell me about what happened today?"

"Umm … well, you know I decided to stay in Florida, so I needed to fix my driver's license. I turned in all the paperwork and had a new picture taken. I was surprised, it's not half bad. Anyway, as I was pulling out of the parking lot, there was an old beater car waiting at the light. I noticed it because it had weird fluorescent paint. When I looked up, I about had a heart attack. I was expecting it to be some teenager on their way to take their driving exam. I never thought in a million years I would come face-to-face with the man who held me prisoner for months."

"Does he have any distinguishing marks? What makes you so certain it was Heath?"

Mariah gulps in a breath as a shudder goes down her spine. "As long as I live, I will never forget the evil in his eyes and the smirk on his face. He wears that dumb expression even when he's asleep. I don't even know why I once thought it was sexy. I couldn't believe it when I saw him driving that car. Heath makes a huge deal about the cars he drives. It's like he derives his sense of identity from them. The more expensive and flashier they are, the happier he is. When he was planning licks, he would choose the marks in part based on the cars in the driveway."

"What can you tell me about the car?"

Mariah bites her lip. "I'm terrible with cars. I should've paid more attention to my grandpa growing up. I remember he used to tell me about the cars in the 70s which blew up if they were hit from behind. I don't think it was that old, but it was super old. It wasn't even a muscle car … it was just an old car — maybe like a Chevy or something. It was black and had one gray door. There was green fluorescent paint which looked like primer."

"Could you see a license plate number?"

She shakes her head. "As soon as I saw Heath's face, I stopped thinking about anything except getting away."

"That's all right. You did a good job with your description of the car. That'll be helpful. Any indication he recognized you?"

Mariah slumps in her chair. "Geez! I hope not. As quickly as I could, I put my car visor down. With the tinted windows and my new short haircut, I don't think he recognized me. I had sunglasses on too. That should help, right?"

I reach out to squeeze her hands. "Mariah, your new look is stunning. But your confidence is even more transforming. Heath, or whatever his real name is, probably figured you would go home to Alabama. He was not expecting to encounter you in Gainesville driving a completely different vehicle during the middle of the day. It probably never even computed in his brain. If he is keeping with his routine, he was probably drunk or high and his senses were dulled."

Mariah leans forward and smiles. "Oh my gosh!

Good point! It's only nine-thirty in the morning. That slug doesn't usually fully wake up until about four o'clock in the afternoon."

"There you go! So, you've given my team some valuable information. I'll pass this on to the fugitive recovery unit."

A pensive look crosses Mariah's face. "You mean you won't be handling this yourself? Are you sure you're not passing the buck? I don't want my case to be forgotten on somebody's desk somewhere."

I flash her a tight grin. "I don't think there's any danger of that. I'll be fully involved in the takedown of Heath and his perverted buddies."

Mariah sits up ramrod straight. "What do you mean? You won't do anything stupid, will you? You're like my only real friend here. I don't want anything bad to happen to you."

"You mean tons to me, Mariah. I never plan to do stupid things. I'll be careful, I promise. But I've got to catch these guys before they hurt anyone else."

CHAPTER FIFTEEN

TOBY

PAULINE TWIRLS IN FRONT of me showing off her outfit. "Do you think I look younger in the miniskirt or the torn jeans?"

The knot in my stomach cinches tighter and my headache pounds as I clench my jaw. "I can't believe you're asking me that."

"Come on! It's a serious question. It's important for the success of this operation for me to look as young as possible."

"'The success of the operation,'" I repeat hollowly. "What about your safety? Does anyone care about you?"

Pauline whirls around and faces me. "*Everyone* cares. We've been over this. Our force isn't as big as Gainesville. Everybody pitches in when we're needed. We're lucky we have the backing of Identity Bank and your resources. But let's face it, my job is dangerous. I knew that going in. Hello! My dad was shot on the job, remember?"

"So why in the heck are you doing this?" I yell. "We are *this* close to catching these guys electronically." I pinch my fingers together to demonstrate. "The risk is so much higher now that Bex Michaels' conviction was overturned on a stupid technicality and he's out pending retrial. Why put yourself out there?"

Undaunted, Pauline pokes me in the chest and succinctly answers, "Because it's my job."

"Not good enough! It's Dylan and Cody's job too, but they're not risking their lives going undercover trying to infiltrate some sick pedophile ring."

Pauline holds up the leather miniskirt and smirks. "Not really Dylan's style, is it?"

"You think this is a joke? These guys are deadly serious! Do you know what it's like to be held captive by one of these creeps?"

"No, I thank everything that is holy I don't have first-hand knowledge of what it's like to be a victim. I have a vague idea of what it's like because you, Mariah and countless other survivors have shared your stories with me. It's because I take stories like yours and Mariah's seriously that I can't sit this one out. We have credible evidence the key players are local and actively recruiting victims. I've been working on this case for years, Toby. I can't ditch this assignment simply because it scares you. I have to finish it and get Bex Michaels off the street for good this time."

I blink slowly as her words impact me as if they were physical blows to my body.

"Scared?" I repeat incredulously. "You think I'm just scared? Not even close. Scared doesn't touch what I'm feeling. Scared is what you feel when you go to the bathroom in the middle of the night and you look up and there's a gigantic spider on the wall about to drop on your head."

A chill goes down Pauline's spine. "Yuck! I hate that!"

"Scared is what you feel when you're at the grocery store with five bags of groceries and you can't find your bank card in your wallet and can't remember the last place you used it."

Pauline nods. "Yeah, that's the worst."

I clench my fists and let them go as I rake my hand through my hair. "No! No, it's not the worst! That's what I'm trying to say. Scared doesn't even begin to cover what I feel when it comes to you. Every time we have a task force meeting and we talk about an op where you might come in contact with these sociopaths, it's all I can do to not have an anxiety attack right on the spot. It takes every coping mechanism I've developed over the last few years for me not to either pass out or go off on every person who suggests such an idiotic move."

"But —" Pauline interrupts.

"Wait, just listen to me!" I command as my voice breaks with emotion.

Pauline's mouth snaps shut abruptly as she regards me with wide eyes.

I struggle to soften my tone and sound like a rational human being as I attempt to explain the inner demons she can't possibly understand.

"Ever wonder why I don't usually go out with you all for drinks after we've worked on a case together?"

Pauline shrugs. "I figured you were shy, or pool and darts just weren't your thing — you know like your issue with movies."

I groan before I briefly rest my forehead against hers. "Argh! I hate this! If I tell you the battles I fight every day, you'll turn and run as fast as you can — and I wouldn't blame you for leaving."

"What are you talking about? Why would I do something like that?"

"Why wouldn't you?"

"Do you actually think I'd be dumb enough to leave because you tell me the truth?"

"That's exactly the type of thing I've been trying to explain. My whole life has been a series of lessons which taught me people have a hard time handling the kind of truth I dish out. First, I trusted somebody who said they were my friend and now I'll spend a lifetime dealing with the consequences of that. I haven't been able to have a normal relationship since then. I'm not even sure I'm capable of love."

"I'm willing to gamble that's not true. I see your love in action every day. I'm not willing to throw in the towel because things might get difficult."

"This is a little more than just 'difficult'. We have huge issues to sort out between us. Our challenges might get bigger than we can handle. Tougher than us."

"I can handle tough. I made it through the police academy with honors. Can you imagine how much hazing goes on when you're the daughter of a cop and your colleagues think you got there because of who you're related to?"

"I'm not talking about your regular everyday toughness here. I am more than a little scared. When I go home and think about what you have planned, I can't breathe. Sometimes, I have to get into the shower and scrub every inch of my skin with scalding water and every soap I own because I swear I can feel Rapture's hands on my body. I scream until I have no voice left because all I see is Bex Michaels or one of his minions violating you in the same way."

A tear slides down Pauline's face as she whispers roughly, "Why didn't you say anything?"

I let loose with a surprised burst of laughter. "What do you mean? I've said plenty! I've practically thrown a tantrum in the middle of every task force meeting we've had lately. I think I've made my feelings crystal clear. Should I have sent up smoke signals?"

Pauline chews on her bottom lip for a moment. "No, of course not. I thought you were being like everyone else who treats me like glass or like I'm some bimbo who can't remember my lines from a high school play. I was so intent on proving you wrong, I didn't stop to listen to the real reasons why you didn't want me in on the op."

I reach out and grasp her hands between mine. "Look, I know you're one of the smartest people I've ever met. If this wasn't my nightmare scenario, you'd be the first officer I'd call. But I love you too much to purposely send you into a situation where I know you could get hurt — or God forbid — taken away from your family for a decade and forced to lead the kind of degrading life I did. I could never forgive myself. I can't design enough high-tech gadgets to protect you from the truly evil. Do you understand that?"

Pauline nods. "I'm just trying to do my job. I swear, I never meant to torture you in the process. Let me see what I can do. Whatever I decide, we have to figure out how to square the fact that I love you with the reality that sometimes I have to put myself in overtly dangerous situations to rid the streets of filthy dangerous scumbags."

"I get that. But do you always have to be the one out front leading the charge?" I ask as I hug her close.

I can barely hold my eyes open as I stand in line and wait for coffee at Tough Breaks. When I reach the counter, I do a double-take when I see Casey standing there in a hairnet and apron.

I blink and clear my throat. "I know I slept worth beans last night, but don't you work somewhere else?"

Casey grins. "If you talk to Savannah, she'll tell you I have more than one job most of the time. But today, I am riding the nostalgia train and helping out a friend. This joint used to be mine. So, I couldn't resist stepping behind the counter for a while. What can I get for you?"

"I need an extra-large cup of espresso with a couple of double shots of caffeine."

Casey tilts his head and studies me. "You okay? Not your usual order."

A slim Latina woman walks up behind Casey and hugs him from behind. "I owe you a dozen of your favorite pastries, Boss Man. You're a lifesaver."

Glancing back, he retorts, "Natalie, I'm not your boss man anymore. You and your mom bought this business from me and made it even more successful than it was. Did you have to buy new tires?"

She shakes her head. "No! It turns out there was some manufacturing problem with the valve stem. They replaced all four for free! I couldn't believe it. I guess that's why my mom always hassles me to turn in the warranty card. Thanks for filling in so I could get it taken care of."

After Casey hands me my espresso, I sit down on a stool in front of the counter and take a sip. I grimace as the bitter brew hits my tongue. Natalie covers her giggle with her hand as she asks, "Everything all right over there?"

I heave a weary sigh. "No, not really. But it's not actually your deal, so thanks for the coffee."

Turning to face Natalie, Casey asks, "You good if I leave?"

Natalie grabs an apron and places it over her head and ties it in the back. "Sure, I knew you couldn't handle the tough stuff for long," she teases with a wink. "Go back to your cushy office job. See if I care."

"You have no idea how many days I sit in my office job and wish I was back behind this counter. Don't get me wrong, I love what I do, but I also loved owning Tough Breaks."

"I'm just giving you a hard time. I know you loved this shop like your baby, but I also know you serve a bigger purpose now. Go help your friend," Natalie says as she pats him on the shoulder.

Casey grabs his ever-present carafe and walks around the counter. Before I know it, he is inches away from my barstool. "Wanna go for a walk?"

Startled, my jaw drops open for a moment while I collect my thoughts. "Am I going to be billed for this counseling session?" I ask defensively.

Casey's eyebrow raises. "Well, I suppose I could if you really want me to, but I was simply checking in with you as your friend."

"Oh." I respond, feeling chagrined. "I could use one of those. My brain is thinking in circles. It's like I'm trapped in my own logic and don't have any perspective. I could use a friend."

"Well, what are we waiting for? Let's get out of here."

Waves of claustrophobia hit, I tug at the collar of my shirt and then fiddle with the zipper on my jacket. "Do we have to go back to your office? I'm too antsy to sit inside."

The corner of Casey's mouth twitches up and laugh lines appear. "Could be your choice of beverage this morning. That stuff would rev up anyone's engine."

I take another swallow and nod. "Good point. But it's more than that. It's been a rough few days."

A look of sympathy flickers in Casey's eyes. "Flashbacks?"

"Unrelenting,"

Abruptly, Casey jerks his head to the side indicating I should follow him. He takes a pocket knife and unlocks a wrought-iron gate which leads to a private patio behind a business. "What are we doing?" I ask as he takes the covers off some patio furniture.

He shrugs. "You said you didn't want to be inside, and this is the most private spot I know of around here."

"Okay, I said I was antsy, I didn't say I want to be arrested for trespassing. You know my girlfriend is a cop? That would be totally embarrassing."

Casey grins. "Lucky for you my wife has a tendency to get claustrophobic too. That's why she created this outdoor studio so she could people watch and paint at the same time."

I look around the quaintly decorated patio. "This is Savannah's place? I thought she worked at Uncommon Paths with you."

"She does. She helps with art therapy and peer-to-peer interactions, but first and foremost, she is an artist. That's how we met. I was nosy and pushy. I made a pest of myself until she fell in love with me."

I flop down in one of the padded lawn chairs. "Love is hard. I always figured you guys had it easy compared to being single, but now I understand why everybody looks stressed out all the time."

"So it's like that with Pauline now, is it?"

I throw my hands up in the air. "I don't know! I want it to be — or at least I think I do."

"What's wrong? Doesn't she feel the same way about you?"

"No, that's not the problem. Pauline says she loves me. But I don't know if I can believe in love because I'm not sure I'm even capable of loving her back like a normal person. I think Rapture Borges stole that part of me."

"You know, this isn't the first time I've heard someone say something like that," Casey observes.

I have to bite back my scoff. "I bet not since you're a counselor."

"Actually, I'm not even talking about my job. It took Savannah a long time to conquer all the negative thoughts put in her head by her abusers. She truly believed she was broken and would never be whole again. She had it in her mind that she wasn't good enough for me. The thing is, she couldn't have been more wrong. I love her despite the scars on her soul. They are part of who she is, and they make her beautiful."

"I have scars all right, but they don't make me beautiful. They make me reactive and angry. They make me terrified to let my girlfriend do her job. They make me scared to believe that love is real."

"Your scars are deeper than most, but no one enters a relationship without baggage. I'm sure it's something you and Pauline can work through."

"How can we work through it when the thing which makes her tick is the very thing that paralyzes me with fear?"

"That's a very good question. If compromise is not an option, you have to decide if your love is bigger than your fear."

Chapter Sixteen

Pauline

My dad peers over the top of his computer screen as I nervously gather my purse and cell phone. "You look nice. Hot date or something?"

I sigh as I walk over and sit down beside him. "Or something pretty much sums it up. I'm supposed to see Toby tonight even though he hasn't contacted me in weeks."

"Uh-oh. Trouble in paradise?" my dad asks as he adjusts his glasses.

"Probably. We seem to be at odds over my job — or maybe even my personality. I'm not sure I can change either, so I don't know what to do.

"That's funny, I never got the impression from your young man that he expects you to be anything but yourself."

I nod. "Most of the time it's probably true. But he doesn't approve of my approach to a current project we're working on together. One of our key suspects just got released from jail because of a stupid evidentiary issue and Toby is freaking out more than usual. He thinks it's too dangerous for me to do my job now."

My dad's eyes twinkle. "I've had that conversation a million times or two in my lifetime."

"Really? I always got the impression Mom completely supported your decision to be a cop."

"Supported? Absolutely. Embrace the potential violence? Never. She hated it every single day. Even though the circumstances of my retirement were not what any of us wanted, the fact that it took me out of the field made your mom the happiest woman on the planet."

"How did you guys handle the stress? Sometimes, I think Toby wants to call it quits because of what I do. He thinks I'm reckless and take risks with my job just because I'm afraid to be told I can't."

Hiding a snicker, my dad leans back in his chair. "Seems like Toby has you pretty well pegged."

"What do you mean? You taught me to be a great cop."

"I did. I wonder if I did you a disservice. Maybe you're more confident than you should be for your years of experience."

"That's just dumb, Dad!" I insist. "How is teaching me to be strong and capable in my profession a disservice?"

"Think about it. You are superbly confident in your training and your background. You know your skills will get you out of any jam. Unlike some new officers, you don't second-guess your decisions often. I'm just saying that maybe I taught you too well and it comes at the expense of an innate sense of caution as a beginner."

I chew on my bottom lip. "Toby wonders why I

always have to be the one leading the charge. I figured it was my personality, but maybe you're right."

"Police work is tricky. You have to be decisive but at the same time keep your mind open to other ways to do your job. I don't know what's happening right now, but I do know you. You are a fine cop. I couldn't be prouder of you. But, my dear daughter, you have a giant chip on your shoulder. Maybe it's time to let it go and stop trying so hard to prove yourself. The people who matter already know you are amazing. Everyone else can sit on it and twirl."

"Daddy!" I gasp. "Why don't you tell me how you really feel?" I add with a chuckle.

"Look, sweetie. I worked with women on the force for a long time. Most of the time, it's not a problem. But there will be some people you can't convince no matter how hard you try. So, my advice would be to stop throwing yourself at moving trains like Superman and just do your job. It sounds like you have a lot more than your personal reputation at stake here."

I bow my head. "I have so much to lose. I don't even want to think about it."

My dad leans over and cuddles me against his chest. For a minute, it's easy to forget I'm not a preschooler with a skinned knee. "As headstrong as you are, Pauline, you always do the right thing. I know it's hard to see your way right now, but I have a feeling about you and your Prince Charming. Neither of you throw in the towel easily. I don't expect this to be any different."

"Thanks Dad. That's exactly what I needed to hear."

There is a scowl on Toby's face as I reach the booth and set my purse down. My heart drops to my toes. All the good feelings inspired by my dad's cheerleading session evaporate into thin air. Maybe Toby has decided love isn't enough to save our relationship.

Toby springs to his feet. "You're late. I was afraid something happened to you or maybe you just didn't want to come."

My face turns hot. "Oh, I'm sorry. I didn't mean to worry you. I should've texted. My dad wanted to talk, and the time got away from me."

Toby's expression abruptly changes. "Is Desmond okay?"

"He's fine. I simply wasn't watching the clock."

Toby swallows hard. "Look, I don't mean to jump down your throat. This is one of my hang-ups. I don't like to wait. I spent years waiting to be rescued. The clock could never move fast enough. Even though it's been years since I've been a captive, any time I have to watch the clock it sets my nerves on edge."

His words hit me like a roundhouse kick. "If I had known, I would've been more careful. I don't want to hurt you." I stand on my tiptoes and kiss him as I fervently hope this isn't the last time I have the right.

Much to my relief, Toby doesn't resist my kiss and pulls me closer for a long embrace before he pulls away.

"It's this kind of stuff I was telling you about. I can be fine until I'm not. It's like whatever happened to me scarred my soul. I'm not sure I can come back from that."

I pull Toby back to the table and sit with him as we hold hands. "Toby, it's a small adjustment. Now that I know about it, I'll be more careful to be on time or let you know if I have to be late."

Toby shakes his head. "But that's not fair to you, you shouldn't have to live your life on eggshells because I can't deal with life as a normal human being."

I smile. "I don't think it's just us. Let me tell you a funny story about my mom. Christie Lawrence is one of the most capable women I know. She is fierce! That is, until she sees a spider. She is so deathly afraid of spiders, she once called my dad from the middle of a chair in the kitchen because she was afraid to set foot on the ground. My dad had to leave a briefing to go kill a spider so my mom could breathe comfortably in her own house."

The corner of Toby's lips turns up in a reluctant smile. "Since I have my own list of anxieties a mile-long, I feel a little sorry for your mom. Was she terribly embarrassed?"

I shrug. "I suppose at first she probably was. But eventually she told the story with such great relish you would think my dad leaving work to kill spiders was far more heroic than all of his police work combined."

"It's a great thing when somebody understands what makes you tick and doesn't judge you for it."

I swallow hard. "Do you think I judge you?" I ask in a shocked whisper.

"Mostly no. Sometimes I think you get impatient with me — but I don't believe you judge me. I'm just afraid someday you might."

"Fair enough. But I'm not perfect either. You're right. Sometimes I'm so eager to prove I can do something I forget about the collateral damage of my decisions."

Toby squeezes my hand. "That's what I wanted to talk to you about."

"Oh my gosh! This is going to be really bad, isn't it?"

Toby looks perplexed. "I don't think so. Why?"

I let out the breath I've been holding. "Because anytime I have heard someone say something like that, they're about to break up with me. I don't want you to break up with me. I love you."

"Oh no … that's not what I meant at all." Toby answers with wide eyes. "In fact, I meant to say the opposite."

My eyes tear up. "Really?"

"Really." Toby clears his throat. "You might have noticed I haven't been around for a few weeks since our last conversation."

"Yeah, it was kinda hard to miss. I was losing hope."

"Sorry about that. It took me longer than I hoped to screw my head on straight. I was trying to wrap my brain around the concept that I could be terrified for you and still let you be who you need to be."

"But you're not the only one who needs to change —" I try to interrupt.

Toby holds his hand up to stop me.

"I need to say all of this to you before I lose my nerve. I've decided our love is bigger than my fear. After my brother and Kendall rescued me, I promised myself I would not waste one more minute of my life on Rapture and the damage she caused me."

Toby pauses to take a drink of water. "Unfortunately, it was harder to follow my plan than to make it. The aftereffects of my kidnapping still make my life difficult. But after spending time away from you, I realize that's not a situation I can handle. I'd rather live with the fear and have you by my side than play it safe and be alone."

I blink back tears. "That is the most beautiful thing anyone has ever said to me. I love you too and I'll try not to rush headlong into situations if there is a safer alternative."

Toby digs in his backpack and pulls out a box the size of a child's lunch pail. "Speaking of safety, I developed this to help keep you safe during your undercover operation with Bex Michaels."

I cautiously open the box as if I am a member of the bomb squad and examine the contents.

"What is this? It looks like some sort of insulin meter or something."

Toby grins. "That's exactly what it's supposed to look like!"

My brows furrow. "I must be more exhausted than I thought. I'm not following."

Toby pulls the device out of the box and attaches it to my upper arm. "You can put it here or you can put it on your thigh. The microphone works either way. This device will allow you to communicate with our team even if Bex and his cohorts take your cell phone. It looks like an attached insulin or pain pump. This is only a prototype, but when we attach it to you, we will put some wires and tape and run a continuous loop of vitals, so it looks like a functioning device that no one wants to touch because it seems a little off-putting."

"Wow! It's really clever. Especially if you can make it look like it's attached to me semi-permanently."

"That's the plan. I'd like to take you to the beach tomorrow to test the prototype in different kinds of weather. Are you up to it?"

"Testing a device to defeat the bad guy? Are you kidding! I'll do that any day in the week and twice on Sunday. Sign me up!"

"I appreciate your enthusiasm, but this is an early product. It might not work exactly like I planned. That's why I want to have you use it to get some hands-on experience."

"I understand. Logistically, it's a good idea to expand the field testing of this before we actually have to use it. But what makes you think Bex Michaels won't simply take it from me?"

"Rumor has it Mr. Michaels had his wisdom teeth out a few years ago and the procedure did not go well. He fears all things medical and practically faints at the sight of blood. We can use his fear to our favor. Why would he want anyone to disable such a delicate medical device? After all, he might break it or something."

I smirk. "Well then, I guess I'll just have to stress how much I bled the last time the device was removed."

For the first time in a while, the stress seems to melt away from Toby as he grins. "Exactly my thought. Great minds think alike."

Chapter Seventeen

Toby

PAULINE LOOKS DOWN IN disbelief as I blend in the last of the stage makeup. "Wow! If I didn't know this device wasn't literally attached to me, I would be totally fooled."

The tips of my ears are hot with embarrassment. "Lucky for me, my sister-in-law, Kendall used to be part of the drama club and knows a little about stage makeup. I have been practicing on my own arms to make sure it looks realistic."

"Well, you definitely got the technique down. I hope it's easy to learn. I don't know how I'll fix it up if the makeup gets damaged."

"It's not hard. It's just a matter of layering."

Pauline's eyes sparkle with mirth. "Oh, I'm good at layering. I do it all the time when I have to disguise the fact I've stayed up too late."

I push a hidden button on the side of the device. When it vibrates against Pauline's arm, she jumps. "When the device pairs with one of your team members, it will vibrate like that."

Pauline's expression sobers. "I guess I need to work

on not reacting or I'll give myself away. Just out of curiosity, how far away will my backup be?"

"I've done some field testing. This thing has a range of a couple of blocks."

"That should make everyone feel a little better about this operation."

"I'll admit, it makes me feel a little better. I hate knowing that Bex Michaels is running loose," I mutter. But we've been over this a million times and I know Pauline isn't going to change her mind. So, I struggle to fight my fears and get my head back in the game, so I can just do my job. I point to a small screen on the device. "See this? If we need to communicate with you, the message will appear here. If you need to disguise the message, push the orange button and traditional readings will appear."

Pauline's eyes light up with hope. "You mean you'll be able to send me love notes while I'm on the inside?"

I lean down and kiss her shoulder. "I don't know if it would be proper for me to get so personal during an undercover operation. But, maybe we can devise a special code or something."

"Speaking of personal, can I shut this thing off when I have to use the ladies room?"

My jaw tightens. "Technically, I suppose you could. I just wish you wouldn't. There's no guarantee something won't happen to you in places which are supposed to be private."

Pauline slowly blinks. "Good point. Well, it's not as if I have a lot of secrets from you. Now, I won't have any, I guess."

"The team will respect your privacy as much as we

can, but we need to be able to monitor what's going on in there to keep you safe."

"Safe. That's the whole point of this, right?"

I nod.

Pauline kisses me on the lower side of my jaw. "Then I trust you. Shall we take this baby for a spin and see how it works?"

I stick my earpiece in as Pauline sprints down the beach. I hear her giggle and mimic a popular phone ad as she says, "Can you hear me now? Can you hear me now? Can you hear me now?"

I laugh at her exuberance as I take out my tablet and type a response.

"Wow! That feels weird. I'll need to practice in front of the mirror to make sure I don't give it away," Pauline responds as she stops to read the message I sent.

"You'll get it. You're the best," I quickly type. I raise the binoculars so I can see her.

Pauline draws in a deep breath. "As much as I'm jazzed about having a backup team during this operation, having you as my cheerleader might be the best perk of all."

I send a smiley face.

"I need to practice around other people. Just roll with the punches, okay?"

Before I can respond, Pauline joins a game of beach volleyball being played with a large brightly colored ball.

"Hey guys, I noticed you're short a player. Mind if I join? I'm Pauline, by the way."

The teenagers turn around and stare. "Yo, Pauline,

know anything about volleyball? We're making it up as we go along," a young girl asks as she takes in Pauline's lithe, athletic figure.

Pauline shrugs. "I played a little in high school. It's been a while, but I think I can figure it out."

A lanky guy with long hair points to Pauline's upper arm. "Is your insulin pump in the way there? My sister usually puts hers on her abdomen. Yours looks a little different, though."

"Yeah, it's a new prototype. I am in a medical trial. It hasn't been released to the public yet. It's pretty rugged. I'll just be careful."

"Just a sec, I have an idea." The guy runs to his backpack and grabs a bandanna. "I swear this is clean. I washed it last night."

"I'm impressed. Most of the guys I went to college with pretended they didn't know how to do laundry," Pauline jokes.

"My mom would kill me if I pulled something like that." The guy ties the bandanna over the device. I am a little concerned, I haven't tested the conductivity under clothing. I breathe a sigh of relief when I hear him say, "It's not much, but it should provide a little protection. We can get a little wild while playing."

A kid with red hair shouts, "Hey! She looks like a good athlete. Maybe she should play on our team since we're losing."

Pauline throws her head back and laughs. I love that sound. Her whole face lights up and she goes from being quietly beautiful to absolutely stunning.

"You guys may be overestimating my skills. It's been a while since I played. I'll tell you what, just to even the score I'll switch sides with every game. Sound fair?"

"Yeah, I guess. At least our side will get a chance to see how you play first," the redhead concedes.

As soon as Pauline steps on the court, the players rearrange themselves. "What are you doing?"

"Oh, we probably should've told you nobody on our team can serve worth crap, so we are hoping you can bail us out."

"What did I get myself into?" Pauline murmurs softly as she covers her mouth by pretending to wipe away sweat. "I hope this thing can handle some sweat."

Her comment makes me grin for a couple of reasons. First, I am relieved I can hear her when she speaks under her breath. This will be helpful to the operation. Second, if I know anything about my girlfriend it's that she is fiercely competitive. Those poor teenagers don't know what a beast they've just unleashed.

Pauline shrugs and throws up her hands. "Okay, don't say I didn't warn you. I'm not even sure I remember how to serve."

Someone tosses Pauline a ball. She tests it by throwing it up in the air a couple times before she settles into the stance of a server. "Here goes nothing," she says before she serves a perfect shot over the net.

After the active group of teens finishes playing the point, the girl from the other side comments, "I don't know what just happened, but I feel like you under-reported your skill level."

Pauline grins. "It's early yet. You just haven't seen me screw up."

The other team serves, and Pauline jumps up to hit

the ball. When she comes down, she collides with another player. She automatically clutches her arm where the device is located.

The girl with brown curly hair looks horrified. "Oh my gosh! I didn't mean to hurt you. Are you okay?"

Pauline makes a show of peeking under the bandanna. "I think everything is fine. Our little mishap didn't screw anything up."

"Wow! I'm surprised you're not bleeding. When my sister swaps out her insulin pump, putting in a new cannula makes her bleed."

Pauline places her hand over the bandanna. "So far, I've been lucky. But I'll keep that in mind."

A cell phone rings in the background. After a few moments, one of the teenagers says, "Hey, we gotta go. My mom will be here soon. Thanks for playing with us. It was fun."

Pauline reaches up to give them all high-fives. "It was fun. If I see you guys around, we could play another round." She reaches up to take off the bandanna.

The tall guy with long hair shakes his head. "Don't worry about it. I have a ton of them. Keep it as a souvenir and a reminder that you're a wicked good volleyball player."

Pauline flashes him a smile. "I'll treasure it forever."

After the group leaves, Pauline jogs back toward me. "So what did you think? Could you hear anything?"

I gather her in a tight hug. "Yeah, everything worked like we planned even with the unexpected twists you threw in. You were amazing! If I didn't know better, I would've guessed you've known those kids your whole life. I wish I had your people skills. I see now why everyone says you are a master at undercover operations."

"Don't sell yourself short, Toby. I could never come up with the creative ideas you have for this op. This solution was genius. If you ever had any doubt your device could pass muster, this should wipe them away. They totally bought it."

I nod. "They did — but I wonder if I should build in some capacity for you to 'bleed'. I didn't think about the device potentially causing you more injury if it was jostled."

Pauline takes off the bandanna and sticks it in her back pocket. "Given the alleged phobias of our perpetrator, it may not be a bad idea. I guess it depends on how realistic you can make the blood."

"Between me and the team at Identity Bank, we can make Bex Michaels faint like a Victorian schoolmarm."

"Sounds good to me. Maybe he'll hit his head and develop a conscience."

Chapter Eighteen

Pauline

"How was your weekend, Rookie? You're looking a little sunburned," Cody teases as he salutes me with his coffee. "Must be nice to have time for R and R."

I wrinkle my nose. "It wasn't all rest and relaxation. Toby and I got some work done."

Dylan winks at me. "Oh, is that what we're calling it now?"

I shrug out of my jacket and show them the device attached to my arm. "Oh, shut up! We really were working. We went to the beach to test Toby's new surveillance device. It works great. The special-effects makeup is even waterproof, so we were able to play in the water."

Cody walks over to me as he whistles softly between his teeth as he examines my arm. "When Toby described the concept to me, I was totally skeptical. I figured there was no way it would look realistic. I am happy to say I was completely wrong."

A warm feeling of pride washes over me. "I know! I'm wearing it, but I'm still blown away. Toby is so shy and self-deprecating, it's hard to guess he is such a genius."

Toby enters the room and looks embarrassed when all eyes are on him.

"Did we miss something?" Tristan asks.

"Oh, we were just having a Tobias Payne fan meeting while we waited for you," Cody responds. "You hired some serious talent. There are many agencies who could use Toby's skills. I am surprised no one's tried to recruit him out from under Identity Bank."

Tristan rolls his eyes. "Nobody says they haven't."

Wide-eyed, I look over at Toby. "Is this true? Why didn't you say something?"

Toby shrugs. "I like it at Identity Bank. Not all jobs would give me the flexibility to move from one coast to the other at will."

My heart rate increases. "You're moving?"

"Why wouldn't I? You're here. Not having you in my life is not an option."

"You guys sound like Lauren and me. We had to make tough decisions too," Dylan adds.

Toby clears his throat. "Speaking of tough decisions, we have to make one as a team."

My heart feels like it slammed to a stop. "What do you mean?" I ask with trepidation.

Toby runs his hand through his hair. "You've been looking for a way to infiltrate Bex's group. I think I found a way. I have been monitoring Bex Michaels' websites. He seems to be meeting a few of his talent recruits at the skate park this evening."

"Does my undercover alias know about this event?" I ask. "I've been swamped with reports and haven't had a chance to look."

"Audra Beckle knows he's having some sort of event. She told him she would try to make it if busking was slow."

"Audra?" Cody asks with a smirk. "You come up with the most interesting names for your undercover characters."

"What? Don't you think Audra sounds like a name destined for stardom?"

"Destined for something," Toby mutters under his breath.

"You still have concerns about the op?" Dylan asks with a concerned expression.

"Always, but I think they're manageable now. The device works flawlessly. I've seen Pauline in action. If anyone can pull off Audra, it's her."

"So where will the backup team be located?"

"Fortunately, I have a friend who owns a food truck. We can park it close and fit right in."

Tristan chuckles. "I see a problem with that plan. Won't people be expecting food?"

Toby shakes his head. "That's what gave me the idea. The other day I went to go get food and my buddy's truck was having trouble with the cooking source. He had an out of order sign on the food truck. We can do the same."

"Brilliant. That should give you guys enough room to work and still stay close," I comment. "Knowing you'll be around makes me a little less nervous."

"Yeah, Rookie. That's how it's supposed to work

when you actually tell your teammates you have an op," Cody remarks.

I bury my face in my hands. "Am I ever going to live that decision down?"

Dylan laughs out loud. "Probably not. Your stunt is pretty legendary."

"Yeah, Dylan's right. The only way you're going to bury that story is if you have a better takedown."

I cough to clear my throat. "Well, I guess I better warm up my singing voice, so Bex notices me."

Toby's jaw tightens and it looks like he wants to argue. Instead, he places his hand on my shoulder.

"If you need help, just ask. We have your back."

I twist some daisies in my hair before I brush off the seat of my impossibly minuscule jean shorts and sit down. I pull out my guitar and leave the case open as if I'm busking.

As I look around, I murmur, "It's pretty quiet. Are you sure something is going down tonight?"

The device on my arm vibrates in three short bursts. It's the signal Toby and I worked out for "yes".

I pick up my guitar and start to sing, *Hallelujah* with a soft country twang.

Off to my left some skateboarders are throwing some tricks.

After a few minutes of playing, a guy comes into the park carrying a video camera. It is similar to what you would see a news crew use. A chill travels up my spine. It's all I can do to remember the words of the Dolly Parton song I'm covering.

Bex Michaels isn't hard to recognize. I have been studying his mug shot for days trying to figure out how a hearsay ruling from the judge could put such a creep back on the street. If I have my way, we'll have enough evidence to build a whole 'nother case against him.

I move on to a Jewel song as I keep an eye on the perp. My pulse is racing as I try to disguise my reaction when he goes up to a group of young teenagers and starts to film them. One young girl is grinning with absolute adoration. I look at him critically. I know so much about him that he is absolutely repulsive to me. However, he is a striking, exotic-looking man. His hair is jet black and his eyes are a piercing blue.

On the fourth song of my set, Bex Michaels wanders over and drops a twenty in my guitar case. My eyes widen for a second, but I continue to sing my Kelsea Ballerini cover.

"Hey, you been here before? You look familiar."

I shake my head before my song concludes. "No. This is my first time here."

"Are you sure? I swear you remind me of someone."

I shrug. "Coulda been my cousin. She's the one who recommended this place for busking."

Bex looks skeptical. "Where you from?"

I make a show of retuning my guitar. "Here and there. My dad was military, so I'm used to living everywhere and always being the newcomer."

"Well, you got a set of pipes on you, for sure. What's

your name?"

"Audra Beckle."

"Audra from everywhere, how would you like to become a big star?"

I grin eagerly. "You mean like *American Idol*?"

Bex puffs up. "What I have to offer is better than any network television show. You can be in control of your own destiny with me. I am an award-winning photographer." He pulls out a card and hands it to me. "You can check out my work on the website."

"Really? You could make me a big star even though no one has ever heard of me?"

"I sure can. You see those skateboarders over there? A couple years ago, I helped one of them break into the big time and get to the X Games."

"I don't want to be in the X Games, I want to be a famous singer like Carrie Underwood."

"Oh, I can do that too. A producer found one of my videos and now that girl is starring in an off-Broadway play."

I study his card. "What would I have to do? I'm tired of busking for pennies."

"I'll tell you what I'm going to do for you just because I love your voice so much. If you come to my studio, I'll cut you a small demo tape and video you can use for tryouts if you want."

I frown. "I don't know you. Anybody can say they're a producer. That doesn't mean you're not bogus."

Bex whips out his phone and pulls up a website. "I'm not bogus! You can check out all these videos here and know I'm the real deal."

I take his phone from him and make a move. After a few moments, I exclaim, "Oh my gosh! I'm so sorry. Your phone is different than mine. I don't know what I just did."

I can practically hear his teeth grinding before he says, "It's all right. I got it."

"So, you're saying this demo tape or video won't cost me any money? As you can see, you are the only paying fan I've had all day."

"You have a very rare talent, I believe in you. For you, I'll do the demo for free. So, when you make it, you can come back and pay me what it's worth."

I chew on my bottom lip. "Why would you do that?"

"Let's just say I have a nose for talent. And I think you have what it takes to be a star. I'm willing to take a gamble on you. So, what do you say? You want to work together?"

I avert my gaze to the ground. "I don't know. It's a lot to think about can you give me your phone number and I'll call you?"

Bex cringes. "Oh, I'm sorry, I'm on a strict timeline. I have to leave town to work a gig. If we're doing this, it has to be tonight."

I look around and point to my guitar. "What about my gig? I gotta eat tonight."

"Don't worry about it. I'll take care of you. My girlfriend might even be over with her kids."

I grin. "Oh, I like kids. I used to babysit all the time."

"Okay then. We're set. I can't wait to make this demo tape with you. Just think of it, you'll have video footage to use in your first music video. You know, where it all started —"

"Are you sure? This seems almost too good to be true."

"Relax. What's the worst that could happen? If you don't like the video, just don't use it."

"I won't be by myself? There'll be other people there?"

Bex nods vigorously. "Oh sure. People come in and out of my place all the time. My pad is like the local hangout."

I suddenly grab my eye.

"What are you doing?"

"I think I got something in my eye. I'm going to go check it out in the bathroom. I'll be right back."

Before he can say anything, I sprint toward the restroom.

"I hope you guys are in range, because we're about to take this to another location," I murmur in the direction of my upper arm.

Toby sends me a message via the device. "Okay, be careful. Send 911 if necessary."

"You know, I am a trained officer. Why does everyone forget that?"

Another message flickers across my screen. "Didn't forget. Love you."

Chapter Nineteen

Toby

Dylan pats me on the shoulder. "If you're going to get her through this, you have to breathe. If you pass out, you'll compromise the operation."

I unclench my jaw and focus on taking a deep breath. "I know. This is just so hard. She is getting in the car. From what I can tell, it's an older Pontiac Firebird. Possibly yellow in color."

Cody addresses me over the radio. "I've got eyes on her."

"Can your car keep up?"

"You're funny. You've ridden in my Mustang. You know darn well I can keep up with anything."

"Whatever you do, keep up with Pauline. I don't want him to disappear with her."

"Understood, Toby. Everyone on the team is watching out for Pauline."

A chime sounds on my computer and I open an additional window and quickly read the contents.

"Heads up guys! Bex has company. He's talking to

someone about fresh meat."

"Just when I thought these guys couldn't get any creepier," Cody grouses.

"Whoever he's texting with is really excited about the prospect," I answer glumly.

"There is not enough antacid on the planet to make my stomach okay with that kind of news," Dylan adds.

"You and me both. I told her this was a bad idea."

"I know it's easy to be overprotective because Pauline looks fragile, but she's anything but weak. She can think her way out of any tough spot better than officers with decades more experience," Cody responds. I hear rustling on the other end of the radio. Then Cody announces "Okay, we're wheels up heading north on Park Street."

My palms are sweaty as I watch the transponder I installed in the device blip across the screen. For several minutes, all I can do is watch as Bex Michaels takes my girlfriend to the middle of nowhere. I'm thankful she consented to the device. At least we have some sort of communication with her, but I have never felt more helpless in my life. I wasn't this stressed-out when my own safety was at risk.

At last, the dot on the computer stops. I hear Pauline in my ear. She coughs to cover the sound as she says, "Tan house 485."

"What are you doing back there?" Bex Michaels demands.

"Just tying my shoe," Pauline answers.

I can almost hear the sneer in his voice as he says, "Wouldn't worry about it. You're not going to have your shoes long anyway. Come to think of it, you're not going to be wearing anything soon."

"I thought you said we were going to make a demo tape?" I don't know if the quiver in Pauline's voice is just acting or if she's really terrified.

"If you're a good girl, we might. But I have other plans for you."

"Other plans? I didn't agree to do anything else. Please let me go back home."

"It's too late. You're here now, so just chill out."

"I don't want to be here. I want to go back home. Please take me home."

"You'll leave when I say you leave."

I hear Pauline gasp as there is a struggle.

"Okay, stop hurting me. I'm getting out of the car. All I wanted was a demo tape. I don't understand why you're doing this."

"You'll soon find out."

I turn to Dylan. "That sounds really ominous. Please tell me Cody has eyes on her."

"I do. She didn't send the distress signal, so she doesn't want us to pull the plug," Cody answers.

Dylan studies me. "Are you sure you want to listen to this? It could get dicey quickly. I know I wouldn't want to hear Lauren go through something like this."

I grit my teeth and take a deep breath through my nose. "I know — but not knowing what's happening to her would be far worse for me. I promised her I would be part of the backup team. She's counting on me to be her lifeline."

Dylan lays his hand on my shoulder. "Okay. I get it.

But if this is too much for you, let me know. I can't pay attention to your reactions and respond to what Pauline needs if things escalate dramatically."

"I can do that. Cody, what street is the house on?" I ask.

"Yonder Court Drive."

"Give me a couple minutes to see what I can get. I never realized how important my hacking skills would be until now."

My fingers fly across the keyboard as I pull up websites and crosscheck them against the information we have on Bex Michaels' cell phone.

I let out the breath I've been holding when I pull up a schematic of the house. "Cody, it looks like there's a sliding glass door in the back and a door that leads out to the garage. If worse comes to worst, there's a large picture window in the front."

"Got it. Can you send me the file?"

"Sure thing," I answer as I forward the blueprints to the rest of the team.

After a few moments, an idea hits me. Thank goodness for Tristan and his expertise in surveillance systems. I run the program Tristan developed to find weaknesses in wireless surveillance systems.

"You guys aren't going to believe this!" I exclaim, practically jumping out of my chair.

"It must be something good," Dylan comments as he watches me type as if I was possessed.

"For someone intent on leading a life of crime, Mr. Michaels is incredibly lax about his security. I'm in."

"You're in where?" Cody asks.

"It seems that Bex has an extensive wireless surveillance system — complete with video cameras. I can now see what he sees."

"Holy sh —" Cody exclaims. "I always knew you were a Wonder Boy, but this is beyond."

"Any way you can share access with Cody?"

"Working on it. I don't want to give away my access, so I have to proceed with caution."

"Even if you can't, your access will help keep Pauline safe."

"That's what I'm here for."

Chapter Twenty

Pauline

Out of the corner of my eye, I look around to see if I can find the backup team. Cody is good when it comes to being invisible and today is no exception. My heart pounds. I hope he didn't lose me.

As we walk up the drive, I notice three cameras. "What's with all the cameras? Am I being watched?"

"You could say that," Bex answers with something short of a maniacal laugh.

"That's weird. Why would you need all those cameras? This house looks like it's in the middle of nowhere."

"Business reasons."

"Oh, I guess I didn't realize making music videos and demos was dangerous."

"I've got some fans who are not so pleased with me right now."

"Sounds scary. I want to be famous, but I don't want to attract stalkers, you know what I mean?"

"Yeah, you never know who you might find on the

Internet."

After we enter the house, my heart drops to my toes when I see him lock the deadbolt behind me and place the key in his back pocket.

I'm surprised by how normal the living room looks. There are nondescript brown couches with a Barbie doll and some matchbox cars strewn about. Just as I'm about to find a place to sit, Bex pulls me toward the kitchen.

"Come on, I'm hungry."

"You want me to make you a sandwich or something?" I offer.

"No, I have other plans for you. Stand over there."

"Okay. But I can make you a sandwich. It's no big deal. I used to work at a sandwich shop in high school. I'm pretty good," I babble.

"Just be quiet for a minute! I can make my own food. You're just like my wife. In fact, you look kinda like her. Strip."

"I beg your pardon?" I stammer.

"I said, take off your clothes."

"I'd rather not. I just came here to make music."

"You're not in charge anymore, I am. Take your clothes off before I do it for you."

"Okay, I can do it," I respond. "My boyfriend is going to be really upset, though. Even he hasn't seen me naked."

"You're a virgin?" Bex asks. I can see spittle form at the corners of his mouth. He is literally salivating at the prospect. My stomach lurches.

"I don't think I should have to tell you that."

Reluctantly, I pull my shirt over my head.

He snickers. "Is that a Mickey Mouse bra?"

"So sue me! I like Disney and I didn't think anyone would see my underwear. It's private, you know —"

I shimmy out of my shorts and stand there. I've worn bikinis which show more skin than my character lingerie. Yet, somehow I feel utterly naked.

"You're a scrawny thing," muses Bex.

"What can I say? I'm never going to be a Victoria's Secret model," I force myself to joke.

He walks around me like I'm a side of beef in a meat locker.

I jump when he yells, "What the eff is that?"

"What?" I ask, looking around.

"What's that thing on your arm?"

I sag in relief as I say, "Oh this? It's a device that helps me clot my blood. I have a rare genetic disorder which makes it impossible for me to make clotting agents. I bleed like you wouldn't believe. I used to have to take six shots a day to keep myself alive. But this pump keeps me from bleeding to death."

Bex Michaels looks a little unsteady on his feet after my announcement. "Just my freaking luck. I gotta get a defective girl. That's going to affect the price."

"The price for what?"

"The price for you. I got clients who will pay big bucks for a virgin. I don't know about you, though, you're scrawny and sick. Get out of my sight. I can't stand to look at that thing. Put your clothes back on."

This is one order I don't have to think about

complying with. I dress as quickly as I can.

"Can I go home now? I won't say anything. I swear. I mean, who would believe me?"

"No! I don't know what the heck I'm going to do with you, but you cannot go home."

Bex moves behind me and starts to push me out of the kitchen and down the hall. He unlocks a door and shoves me in. I stumble across the threshold and he slams the door behind me. I hear the snick of the deadbolt as he locks the door behind me. I don't think there is a more foreboding sound in the world.

When my eyes adjust to the darkness of the room, I realize I'm not alone.

"Do you know what you've just done?"

I shake my head. "No, what'd I do?"

"You pissed him off. That's going to be bad for all of us."

"All of who?"

"Are you telling me you don't know what's happening here?" another voice adds.

"No, I don't have a clue. I just wanted to make a demo tape of my music. That's what he promised."

"Girl, he promised us the world too. Yet here we are."

"Yeah, he was supposed to make me a dancing star — you know like So You Think You Can Dance? He's a freaking liar!"

I gasp. "Oh no! I should've listened to the voice screaming at me in my head. I knew better."

"I'm Tiffany and over there is Shasta. Who are you?"

"I'm Audra. I am the dummy who thought I was coming here to make a music video. So, what's really going to happen to me?"

In the dim light, I can see Tiffany shrug. "We don't know for sure. Shasta overheard Fi Fi talking to Bex about some sort of auction."

"Well crap! This is everything my grandpa ever told me I should watch out for. He was a teacher and never understood why I liked to hang out on the computer. How old are you guys?"

"Crap is right. We've been trying to figure out how to get out of here for days," Shasta responds. "I'm sixteen, but Tiffany here is only fourteen."

"Where you guys from?"

"It doesn't matter now, but I'm from Louisiana," Shasta replies.

"I'm from South Carolina. Can't you tell from my accent?" Tiffany says with a pronounced southern drawl.

"I'm assuming we're still in Florida. That's where I'm from."

"Heck if I know where we are," Shasta grumbles. "I hope somebody misses us eventually. I think that's our only hope of getting out of here."

"Doesn't Bex go to work? What about the window? I'm pretty skinny. I can probably get through there."

"I already tried that. Bars on the windows," Shasta says. Shasta pulls back the curtain and shows me the bars.

"Yeah, we don't know when he's coming or going," Tiffany explains.

I glance at them with a hopeful expression. "He told me he had to go out of town tomorrow on a gig."

Shasta scoffs. "Polly, come on now. You can't believe a word that comes out of that man's mouth. Don't forget that!"

"So we're just stuck here?" I ask, letting the panic show in my voice.

Tiffany nods. "'Fraid so."

"For how long? He can't keep us forever. Someone is going to discover we're here, right?"

"Did you tell anybody you were coming here?" Shasta asks.

Regretfully, I shake my head no. "I didn't think it would be any big deal. I figured I'd hang out at his house for a couple hours and make a tape. My family doesn't really even care what I do because they're mad that I'm a musician. So, they probably won't even look for me because they won't know I'm gone."

Tiffany looks glum. "Yeah, I ran away from home because my mom got remarried and my new stepdad was looking at me funny. Little did I know I was going to end up in a worse situation."

"I hear that," Shasta says. "My dad had a stroke. I thought maybe if I won one of those TV shows, I could get money for him to get better therapy. But I didn't want to let my parents or anybody else know what I was doing in case it didn't work out."

"Oh great! There are three of us here and nobody cares if we're lost," I respond sarcastically. "This is going to suck."

Tiffany gives me a grim smile. "Umm ... There might be more. We can't see who else is in the house. Sometimes we hear other voices besides Bex and his wife."

"Do they feed you?" I ask.

"Depends. If Fi Fi is here, we get food. If it's just Bex, he makes us 'earn' food."

"Do I want to guess what his price is?"

"You don't really want to know. It's gross," Tiffany responds.

"What about the bathroom?"

Shasta points to a five-gallon bucket in the corner. "That's it. If we're lucky, Fi Fi lets us shower. But she watches. It's creepy."

"That's gross! Shasta, what day is the auction supposed to be?"

"I don't know. What day is today?" she asks.

"Today is Thursday."

"Oh no!" Tiffany exclaims. "That means tomorrow is the end of the line. I've heard about what happens to sex slaves. I don't want to do this!"

I walk over and give Tiffany a hug. "Try not to panic. I will think of a way to get us out of here."

"Good luck with that," Shasta replies sardonically. "Tiffany and I have had nothing but time to figure it out. It's hopeless."

"Nothing is hopeless. We can't quit."

"What are we going to do? It's not like we can overpower him or anything. We're as good as sold to some disgusting pedophile," Tiffany laments.

"I don't think so. Sometimes being smart is better than being strong."

Shasta scoffs. "If we were smart, none of us would've been stupid enough to be locked in this hellhole."

"There's a difference between being stupid and trusting in the good intentions of others."

"Not from where I sit." Shasta rolls her eyes at me. "What are you going to do to stop that lying scumbag?"

"I don't know yet. But I'll come up with something."

"Right! I'm done believing people's lies," Tiffany remarks.

"I know it's hard to believe, but just keep your wits about you. I may have a secret weapon or two.

CHAPTER TWENTY-ONE

TOBY

CODY WHISTLES SOFTLY THROUGH his teeth. "Nothing like the Rookie giving us an impossible deadline."

"It's not like she is in charge of what happens to them," I snap defensively.

"No, I don't think Cody meant to suggest that. He's just trying to explain this is a complicated operation," Dylan says.

"Well, no duh!" I reply sarcastically. "That's why it took months to plan."

Dylan studies the big computer monitor in front of me and watches the surveillance footage. It's not great, but it's something.

"Yeah, we did plan. But now we have minors taken over state lines. That complicates things jurisdictionally."

"Screw jurisdictions. We have less than a day to figure out how to get all of them out of there. We don't have time for politics," I insist.

"Wonderboy has a point. By the time we get everyone involved, it might be too late."

"Career suicide anyone?" Dylan jokes.

"Maybe. Still, I know Pauline and my wife would feel much better if I did the right thing instead of the politically expedient thing."

"Okay, anybody want to translate for me? Remember I'm not officially on the payroll of your department. I get to color out of the lines. Tristan gave me explicit permission to do so."

"Loosely translated, it means we're going to do what needs to be done and ask for forgiveness later."

"Sounds like a plan," I respond tersely.

"Hey, you said you hacked into their system, does that also mean you can zoom in on faces?" Dylan asks.

"I probably could — but it's not a good idea because if someone is monitoring the cameras, they will notice the difference in focus."

Cody sighs. "Good point. But it would've been awesome to be able to identify the teenage girls."

"Let me see if I can send a message to Pauline. Maybe she can get the teenagers to walk closer to the security camera."

"Need a close-up. Camera above door," I text into the special application which communicates with her device.

I watch as Pauline looks at her device and nods imperceptibly.

Pauline clears her throat. "I'm thinking things through, but I need to know how big you guys are. Can you come and compare yourself to the door, so I have a visual reference?"

"Okay, but I still think you're nuts. There's no way

out of here," Shasta argues as she gets up and walks closer to Pauline.

"No, come on, there's a point to this," Pauline says as she walks behind Shasta and positions her about two feet from the door. "Look at that, you're about six inches taller than me. Little details like that make a difference."

"I bet I'm shorter than you," Tiffany says. "I'm the shortest person in my family."

"I don't know. Everyone I know thinks I'm a shrimp. Let's compare," Pauline says with a smile.

Tiffany takes Shasta's place. "I can't believe it! This is the first time I haven't been the shortest person in the room."

Pauline grins. "I told you. I may be little, but I'm feisty."

"So, what are we supposed to do? Stand here and will the door to open?" Shasta asks.

Pauline laughs. "It would be cool if we could, but I was thinking more of a planned attack when someone takes a shower. Does he ever let you go to the bathroom in a group?"

"I guess we didn't mention the guns," Tiffany says.

Pauline's body posture stiffens. "Guns? What kind of guns?"

"The scary kind?" Tiffany answers as her shoulders slump.

"Scary long or scary short and small?" Pauline asks.

Shasta answers, "I've seen a Glock and a snub-nosed revolver."

"Well, shoot! That complicates things."

"You think? If it was easy, Tiff and I would've been long gone," Shasta responds with an eye roll.

"Okay, I need you guys to follow my lead but not talk. We're going to have a weird game of Simon says. Do what I do."

I glance over at Dylan with alarm. "What do you think she's doing?"

"If I had my guess, I'd say she's preparing a teenage army. I've seen her teach hand-to-hand combat to the new recruits. It'll be a challenge without words, but it might help save their skin."

"Bingo! Tristan's face recognition software just came back with two IDs," I announce triumphantly.

Dylan looks up from the monitor he's been watching. "Okay, who are we dealing with here?"

"I already knew Bex Michaels was a sicko, but this just confirms it. Tiffany Boyd just turned fourteen less than three weeks ago. She is from Rock Hill, South Carolina. She was reported missing six weeks ago."

"Son of a B —"

"I know! You took the words right out of my mouth. Now I'm sorry I put up such a stink about Pauline being in on this mission. I know you guys went slow because I was having a hard time with it."

I hear Cody's voice in my ear. "Knock it off! Guilt trips don't help anything. You needed the time to develop the device so that we can communicate with the Rookie."

I slump in my chair. "I guess you're right. But I can't

help but think I should've built it faster."

"I know the feeling. I get it every time I go on a case with the Cold Case Squadron. Sometimes, we're just days too late to save someone. Heck, I still feel guilty that we weren't able to save Lauren's sister and she was killed when I was nine. Guilt just goes with the territory. Who is the other victim?"

"Shasta Collins, age sixteen. Her missing person's report indicates she is a track and field star at her high school in Assumption Parish, Louisiana. She has been missing for about eight weeks."

"Oh good. Those skills will help facilitate the rescue."

"Should we notify the parents?" I ask.

Dylan shakes his head. "Normally, I would say yes, but in this case, we can't risk our cover being blown. The last thing we need is a news crew showing up on Bex Michaels' doorstep before we can extract the hostages."

I start to shake. "I've been trying to ignore the fact that my girlfriend is currently being held hostage by a madman with no morals. I don't know how much longer I'll be able to suspend my disbelief and pretend none of this is happening."

Cody's reassuring voice rings through my headphones. "Not much longer. Tomorrow, we extract Pauline, Tiffany and Shasta. We want them all in one location. The auction seems to be the likely place."

"I agree," Dylan adds. "There is an added bonus to that plan. Hopefully, we'll catch some of the perverts who were planning to purchase teenage girls."

"I'm all about that. How can I help?" I ask.

"Right now, we only know that there is an auction planned. We don't know when or where. We have to nail down those parameters before we can do anything," Dylan instructs.

"I'm on it. The unmasking software Phoenix and I have been working on should really help. I might even be able to tell you who the johns are."

Dylan smiles. "Can't ask for much more than that. The more information we have going in, the safer the women will be."

"One more question: how soon can I tell Pauline that the Cavalry is coming?"

"As soon as we have a location and time window," Dylan replies.

"I hope she knows we are on the other end, working to extract her."

"As brave as Pauline is, I'm not sure she would have undertaken this mission if she didn't know you had her back," Cody says through my headphones.

CHAPTER TWENTY-TWO

PAULINE

I AM JERKED OUT of a fitful sleep when a light shines in my face.

"Time for you to get your lazy butt out of bed," a woman commands.

I sit straight up in bed. I move so fast it makes me dizzy.

"Okay, but why?" I ask trying to shake off my mental fog.

"Today is the day we finally unload you."

"Unload me?" I ask, playing dumb.

"Look, I know my husband likes to have you all around to look at. But it takes money to feed you and clothe you, we have to keep turning over the inventory."

Inventory. What a disgustingly simple word for human trafficking.

I look down at my wrinkle clothes. "Like right now?"

A woman I presume to be Felena Hopner scowls at me.

"No, of course not. We have to get you cleaned up

and presentable."

"Presentable?" I press.

Felena lets out a frustrated breath. "Are you learning impaired?"

"I-I don't think so," I stammer.

"Then go get your butt in the shower."

I show her the device on my arm. "I can't do it alone. Somebody has to wrap this for me. Without it, I could die so I can't risk breaking it in the shower."

"Fine. Whatever. What do you need to wrap it?"

"Some Saran Wrap and medical tape," I respond. "I'll need some help from these guys. It works better if two people are helping."

"I'll watch you and do whatever you need," Felena offers.

"Okay, if you wish. But I have to change the cannula. It might get a little bloody."

Felena visibly shudders. "On second thought, just use the girls. Maybe you can teach them some makeup tips."

I glance down at the short denim cutoffs I'm wearing. "What should I wear?"

"Appropriate clothes will be provided."

"For just me — or for everyone?"

Felena just stares at me. "You're not so bright, are you? I just said it's time to change the inventory. That means all of you. I need you all ready in the next hour and half."

"Can't you let Tiffany go? She's just a kid!"

"You don't get it do you? Tiffany is the most valuable

of all of you."

It's all I can do not to throw up on the spot. I concentrate on staying in character when I hear Tiffany sob.

"You guys are a bunch of wusses. Some of these gentlemen are crazy rich. You can be living in the lap of luxury in just a few hours. What is there to complain about?"

I have to bite my tongue. There is so much to complain about that I don't even know where to begin.

"Are these men nice?" Tiffany asks as she tries to collect herself.

Felena shrugs. "Some of them are. A lot of it depends on how you behave."

Felena's phone beeps. She looks down at it and says, "I gotta go. Get whatever you need from the kitchen to cover your thingy, but get cleaned up and dressed. Don't bleed all over my bathroom. My husband has issues with that."

"I'll do my best. Thank you."

She leaves the room and shuts the door behind her. This time she doesn't lock it.

Shasta comes over and whispers in my ear, "I can't believe you got her to do that. What do you have planned?"

"More details later," I whisper.

I grab the hands of both girls and inch my way out of the door into the hallway as I walk between them. "I guess I need you to direct me to the kitchen."

After our scavenger hunt in the kitchen, we take turns brushing our teeth.

"I used to hate taking the time to brush my teeth every day. But, if I ever get out of here, I'm going to brush my teeth ten times a day," Shasta says after she spits out her toothpaste.

Tiffany nods. "Yeah, I never thought I would find myself in a situation where a toilet is a luxury."

After we finish, I turn the sink water on as loud as it will go and start the water in the shower.

I huddle with the girls. "Pay attention! Help is coming, but be on your toes. If I say run, sprint like the world is coming to an end."

Shasta looks incredulous. "Help? How in the world are we going to get help?"

"I'll explain later, but you have to trust me."

"I'm a little short on trust these days," Shasta replies.

"Shas, come on. She got us all in here at once. I think Audra is telling the truth," Tiffany counters.

"You're right. Lead the way. I just hope you know what you're doing, Shrimp."

"Me too. But if we do nothing, the bad guys get their way."

"That can't happen, I haven't even started high school yet," Tiffany wails.

"If I have my way, I'll be dancing at your graduation party."

"I can't wear this! I look like a hooker," Tiffany exclaims as she looks down at the latex minidress.

"I think that's the point," Shasta says as she struggles to pull up tight leather pants.

I examine the impossibly high heels Felena has laid out for us. "These won't work. Let me see what I can do."

"I can't believe they put you in a lame schoolgirl outfit," Shasta says as I tuck in a white blouse to a plaid skirt.

I shrug. "Could've been worse. If my boyfriend could see me in this, he would laugh his butt off."

"Hopefully, your boyfriend will be able to see you someday," Tiffany says.

"Just follow my lead, okay?" I murmur under my breath. Both girls nod.

I pick up the high heel shoes and step out into the hallway. "Excuse me, is anybody here?"

Felena comes down the hall with her cell phone at her ear. "What do you need?"

"I am a really big klutz. I can't walk in these. I'm afraid I'm gonna fall down and trigger a bleeding episode. Can I have some flats, please?"

Felena narrows her eyes. "The men prefer high heels —"

"Probably in most circumstances, but I can barely walk in high heels and Tiffany has never even had them on her feet. If you want to display us properly, we should probably not look like we're going to fall down at any second."

Felena nails Shasta with an evil stare. "I suppose you have issues too?"

Shasta nods. "Actually, I do. I just had knee surgery a few months ago. I'm pretty unsteady on my feet."

Felena scowls. "You all are a pain in my butt. I can't wait until you're gone."

"I'm sorry, but I just don't want anyone to get hurt. It's bad for the inventory, right?"

"Fine. I'll be right back."

As soon as she leaves, I whisper, "Game on."

CHAPTER TWENTY-THREE

TOBY

I SEND UP A cheer when I see Felena Hopner deliver flat shoes. "I knew my girlfriend was smart, but she thinks of everything!" I gush.

Dylan grins. "Like I said, Pauline thinks better on her feet than any officer I know, including myself. It's almost as if she plays these scenarios out in her mind before they even happen. She's prepared for everything."

"Speaking of prepared, is the team in place?"

Cody chuckles in my ear. "Team? You mean teams. This is an all-hands-on-deck situation."

"They know that the auction is supposed to start at noon, right?"

Dylan nods. "Our surveillance team has identified two of the johns already circling the property. I wonder if they're trying to get a glance of the merchandise."

A visceral shudder passes through my body. Merchandise. "My girlfriend is not merchandise. Neither are those other victims."

"Relax, I know that," Dylan says as he pats my shoulder. "Term of art of the industry."

"We need to shut down the whole 'industry'. There should never be a market for children."

"That's why we're here. After this is done, there will be several fewer players in the game."

I roll my eyes. "Yeah, I suppose so if we can keep Bex Michaels in jail this time."

"I made sure we have proper warrants for everything. I even double-checked it with my wife. Sometimes, being married to the district attorney is a helpful thing," Cody answers over the comm channel.

"Your wife is a national treasure. I hope she knows that," Dylan remarks. "Seriously, Toby, the device you created is going to seal this case. They can't argue with the play-by-play Pauline has provided throughout this whole ordeal."

My stomach clenches. "I wish she hadn't had to do that. But I've got the tapes of the whole event backed up offsite."

"It's only a matter of time now until we have this whole situation buttoned up. Just keep the faith," Cody says.

At the moment, I'm cursing the fact that Bex Michaels has so many security cameras. I don't need to see those scumbag pedophiles leering over my girlfriend in four different angles.

Bex Michaels has a microphone from a karaoke machine as he addresses a group of about a dozen men. I'm astonished at the age range. Some of them look barely older than me and others look as if Pauline could be there great-granddaughter. It just confirms what I've always known, pedophiles come in all different shapes and sizes.

"Good afternoon, gentlemen. Now that you've inspected our merchandise, I expect the bidding to be brisk."

"Yeah, every time I come to one of your auctions, my wife wonders what happened to the bank account. I can't exactly explain," a voice from the back says.

Another voice pops up, "Same here. I just tell my wife I was doing some day trading and lost a bundle of money."

"Good line. I'll have to remember that," the guy in the back responds.

"Okay, first up is a spirited little thing. She is scrawny but amusing to deal with. She can entertain you with her music. She has a beautiful singing voice."

"How is she in the sack?" a guy who looks like he's in his fifties asks.

"Oh, I forgot. That's a bonus with this one. She's a little shy in the romance department and she has never been taken."

"What's wrong with her? She's cute. Why hasn't she been snatched up before?"

"Well, part of the reason she's so scrawny is because she has some sort of blood disorder. She apparently has medication to treat it. It shouldn't affect your satisfaction."

"How about it, sweetheart? Are you feisty in bed too?"

Pauline flushes bright red all the way to the roots of her hair.

I have a hunch this is not acting. Pauline is stunningly gorgeous, but she has a hard time viewing herself as anything but a rough and tough tomboy. This has to be excruciating for her.

She takes a deep breath and answers, "I don't know. I guess that depends on you."

"Oh, baby!" the guy says with pure lust in his eyes. "Bex, you were right, this one has quite a bit of fight. It's going to be fun to tame her."

Bex grins. "Not so fast Delancey. You still have to win her in the auction."

The man's chest puffs up. "Not a problem. You know my pockets are deep."

A lanky guy in the back says, "I wouldn't be so confident if I were you, my pockets are deep too."

"With that, let me start the bidding at ten thousand dollars."

Pauline's jaw goes slack and she snaps her head around to look at Bex. I can't blame her. Those amounts are eye-popping. I make pretty good money working for Identity Bank, but even with the size of my paycheck, I couldn't drop that much money. No wonder the guy plays for the bad guys.

The older guy raises his hand. "I'll lay out fifteen grand for her. I need a challenge."

"Twenty," the guy in the back says.

"Ahh man! My pockets are deep, but that's too steep for a play toy."

Bex looks up at the guy in the back. "Congratulations

Smitty, she's all yours."

Shasta looks like she's about ready to tackle someone on Pauline's behalf. Even though Shasta can't see me, I give my head a vigorous shake. We don't need a distraction quite yet.

Bex pulls Shasta in front of him. "This one comes from Louisiana. She knows how to party and she is as strong as they come."

"I like to party," a guy who looks like he's eighty if he's a day, announces.

"Well, your money is as green as everyone else's. What are you willing to pay?"

The older man chuckles. "Preferably as little as possible."

"I'm gonna start the bidding on this one at fifteen thousand."

"I accept," the octogenarian announces.

A young guy in the front counters, "Seventeen grand."

The older guy flinches. "I want to skip all this BS. Twenty-five thousand."

The young guy holds up his hands. "Too rich for my blood."

Shasta looks like she's about ready to pass out. Pauline comes up behind her and helps her to a chair.

Tiffany is cowering in the corner. Felena stalks over to her and pulls her by the arm until she is in the front of the room.

Seeing the terror in Tiffany's eyes reminds me of the boy I was. It's enough to make me want to throw up.

Bex runs his finger down her jaw and lifts her chin. "Okay, as you can see, this one is a little shy. But, she is a sweet investment. For those of you who like them young, this one is for you. I doubt if she's even had her first kiss. I'm going to start the bidding at thirty thousand dollars. Don't try to lowball me. You know how hard it is to get quality merchandise."

A particularly sadistic looking guy shouts from the back of the room. "Forty thousand."

Bex looks around the room expectantly. "Any other bids?"

"I think I want some of this action," a guy who looks like he belongs in a frat house somewhere says.

"You may want in on this, Heath Tanner, but your bank account says about all you can afford are a few burgers and fries. Sit down. You're a spectator today. Anyone else?"

The room is silent as the johns look at each other.

"Okay, Brennan, this one is for you. Try not to put her in the hospital. It's bad for business."

"Oh, but it's so much fun," he counters with a maniacal grin.

"Oscar! I'm serious. We don't need any media attention on our operation. Take it easy with this one."

I buzz Pauline's arm.

Dylan gives the go to the teams surrounding the building.

A half a beat later, I hear Pauline yell, "Run!"

As the extraction team storms the doors and flings them wide open, Pauline is busy challenging one of the men who grabbed Tiffany. I hold my breath as one moment, he appears to have the upper hand. The next moment, he is knocked out cold on the floor. By looking at his face, it looks like Pauline fractured his nose in the process.

"Run, Tiffany, run! These are the good guys."

Tiffany scrambles to her feet and runs toward the exit.

Pauline is so busy making sure Tiffany and Shasta escape, she fails to notice Bex pulled a gun on her.

"I should've known you'd be trouble," Bex growls as he levels his weapon and aims at Pauline's center mass.

Pauline whirls around. "Oh, you want trouble? I can give you some," she says as she performs some sort of martial art move and kicks the gun out of his hand.

One of the extraction team members picks it up.

"Sorry to disappoint you all, but humans should never be for sale. These nice officers will take your names and statements. Don't bother to lie. We already know who you are."

"What kind of bull crap is this?" one of the customers yells at Bex. "Some kind of set up?"

Bex squirms, as one of the officers yanks his arms behind his back and cuffs them. "No, I wouldn't do that. I don't know how they found us."

I place my hand on Bex's elbow and escort him out the back door.

"What the eff happened?" Bex demands. "How did they even know the auction was today?"

I shrug. "I have a very talented team who makes it their business to know yours. I busted you once and it gives me great pleasure to do it again."

"I told Fi Fi you looked familiar. I should've known better. But, you'll never win in court because it's your word against mine and who's going to believe strung out runaways and junkies over me?"

"Yeah, that might be true if I was only a runaway. Unfortunately for you, I'm a highly trained police officer. We have my whole experience on tape. I'll be happy to testify in court about the authenticity. You won't get away on a technicality this time."

"You're such a freakin' liar!" Bex exclaims. "You told me you were a high schooler interested in pursuing music."

"Big deal, I lied. You lied too. But you know what? When I was these girls' age, I wanted nothing more than to sing in Nashville. I had big dreams, just like Shasta and Tiffany — and countless other children you have abused. You seem to take great joy in exploiting the dreams of others. I hope you don't have many dreams for your life because they are about to be interrupted by a very long prison sentence."

"Just shut up! I am a powerful man and you have no idea who you're messing with. This is not over," Bex shouts at Pauline.

"Maybe not. But for today it is. You're going to jail and the girls are going home. I doubt your favorite customers will be coming to any auctions tied to your name anytime soon. I'll take that as a win."

Pauline places Bex Michaels in a patrol car and smacks the top.

"All clear," Cody says in my ear.

I lean back and take the first deep breath I've taken in two days.

"Is it over? Somebody has Shasta and Tiffany?"

Cody answers, "Radio traffic indicates they're already on the way to the hospital."

"Where is Pauline?" I ask as my hands start to shake from the adrenaline coursing through my body.

"I'm on the comm with her. She says she loves you, but she is going to the hospital with the girls since they have no support system."

"Silly me to expect anything different," I comment, rolling my eyes.

"Get used to it," Dylan says. "Being the spouse of a cop is one of the toughest things in the world. I know the Rookie well. She won't be finished until those girls are home with their parents."

"As it should be," I respond. "Still, I can't help but wish she could be two places at once."

"It's funny how much you sound like my fiancé," Dylan comments.

"Does it ever get easier?"

"I'm not sure. You'd have to ask Lauren that. I can just tell you I'm a better cop because I have a soft place to land at home. Be her soft place. This was probably the toughest thing she's ever done."

"I know. That's why I love her so much. It's scary when she rushes headlong into a problem. But if this is the outcome, it's worth it."

"Don't forget to tell her that," Cody instructs. "She needs your approval most of all."

Chapter Twenty-Four

PAULINE

"I'M NOT EVEN SURE what to call you. It's not really Audra, is it?"

I shake my head. "You can call me Pauline."

"Thanks, I was so scared, I thought I was going to pee myself." Tiffany says as she grips my hand from the hospital bed. "Nothing personal, but I want my mom."

"We're working on it, even as we speak. Getting your discharge papers shouldn't take too much longer. I'll tell you a secret. I could really use a hug from my mom right now too."

"Really? You seem like the definition of cool and collected," Shasta responds from the bed next to Tiffany. "I still can't believe you kicked that gun out of Bex's hands. That was badass."

I smile. "Yeah, my dad would be proud. He spent hours drilling me on effective hand-to-hand combat. I haven't had to use it much in my job, but all of my training came in handy today."

"Do you think he'll really go to jail? What about Fi Fi?"

"With the evidence you helped me collect, I have little doubt both of them will end up spending some significant time in jail."

"Evidence? We didn't collect any evidence," Shasta insists.

I point to the device on my arm. "Actually, you did. This is a recording of everything that went on since I crossed paths with Bex Michaels and his wife."

Shasta's eyes widen. "Is that legal?"

I nod. "After Bex Michaels' last conviction was overturned on a technicality, we made sure we had all the proper warrants."

Tiffany leans over to look at my arm. "Can I see?"

I nod. "No reason not to show you, the operation has concluded."

"Concluded seems like such a tame word. We kicked butt and captured a bunch of really scummy guys."

"You have no idea. We've been chasing some of those guys for a long time. They'll be facing more charges than just from this incident."

Tiffany runs her finger around the device as she examines it. "I have to know. Who is sending you love notes and hearts?"

I blush. "That would be my most amazing boyfriend Toby. He kept me sane through this whole thing."

Tiffany cringes. "You mean he heard everything that happened to us? I'm not sure I want anyone to know. It's so embarrassing."

"Don't worry about Toby. Anything he learned during the op will stay private."

"How can you be so sure?" Shasta asks. "Most guys would be talking about this nonstop. I know. I once got my period in the middle of math class. The guys that knew about it still haven't stopped teasing me two years later."

"For a lot of reasons, Toby's not like that. First, he's profoundly shy. More importantly, he's been through something similar to what you guys went through except his kidnapper kept him for about five years."

"Oh wow! He must be really brave to sit by while you were in danger."

I nodded. "It wasn't easy for him. We argued quite a bit about whether it was worth it for me to take the risk."

"I'm glad you won that argument," Shasta says with a wry smile. "Who knows what would've happened to us if you hadn't been there. Our families probably never would've found us."

"I'm glad we worked it out too. But it didn't make it any easier on him to have to listen to everything I went through. Like I said, I have the best boyfriend in the world."

A nurse breezes in carrying clipboards. "Here you go! I have permission to spring you guys from this joint. The doctor wants you gals to follow up with your own doctors when you get home. Sometimes, the shock from these kinds of things can set in later."

After all the paperwork is signed, Tiffany looks at me with tears in her eyes. "Now what? I don't really have a place to go and my mom lives more than six hours away."

"Girlfriend, I'm in the same boat you are. My parents are more than nine hours away," Shasta adds.

"Like I said, we're working on reuniting you with

your families as quickly as possible. In the meantime, is anyone hungry? I know I'm starving."

Tiffany and Shasta both nod eagerly. "Real food for a change? I am so sick of granola bars I'll never look at one again the same way," Shasta comments as she rubs her stomach.

"What do you guys want to eat?"

"Pizza!" Tiffany answers at the same time that Shasta says, "Burgers!"

For a moment, Tiffany looks crestfallen. "You know what? It's been a long time since I had really good fries. Burgers it is."

"How are we going to get there? I don't want to ride in the back of a police car again," Shasta admits. "It's better for the criminals to ride back there."

"I couldn't agree more. But, if I know my very resourceful boyfriend, there is probably a car waiting for us in the parking lot."

The device on my arm buzzes and Tiffany eagerly reads it. "Black Escapade right out front."

"Are you going to keep that weird device after this whole thing? It would be really funny. You could just be in the grocery store and ask out loud, 'Gee, I wonder what kind of ice cream my boyfriend wants?' and you could have an answer right away. No messing with your cell phone."

"That would be funny. But I'm not sure Toby wants his device used that way."

My arm buzzes again. "Works for me. Then I can tell you I love you every minute of every day."

Tiffany's eyes widen as she watches the text scroll

across the screen. "Oh my gosh! You do have the best boyfriend in all the world. That is so sweet!"

Shasta suddenly looks glum. "I don't even know if my boyfriend is going to be around. I was gone for a long time. I wouldn't blame him if he broke up with me since I wasn't there."

"Shasta, you can't do that to yourself. You don't know what things are like back home. He could still be waiting for you to be safe. After all, the only people who know you guys have been rescued are your parents. We asked them to keep it away from the media so you guys would have some privacy."

"Oh, right. I guess I'll try to chill for a while."

"You know, I know this really cool hamburger joint. It doesn't look like much, but they have Parmesan and garlic fries which are to die for."

Tiffany's stomach growls.

"Well, I guess that settles it. We need to go get something to eat."

As we're waiting for our order to appear, Toby comes through the front door. He has a strange expression on his face and I'm not sure if it means he has bad news or what. My stomach lurches to my toes.

He walks up to the table. "You mind if I sit?"

Tiffany's eyes widen with fear. "I don't think so. I don't know you!"

Toby takes a giant step backward. "You're right. I forgot to introduce myself. I am Tobias Payne. I work for

Identity Bank. Along with the police department, we worked together to coordinate your rescue."

"You're Toby?" Shasta asks.

"Umm … yeah. Most people call me Toby unless I'm in trouble with my mom."

"Pauline was just showing us your amazing text message," Shasta says. "Thank you so much for helping her. If it wasn't for her, we would probably be dead."

"You guys had a lot to do with your own rescue. You never gave up even when it seemed hopeless. There's a lot to be said for that."

"OMG! He is as sweet as you say he is," Tiffany gushes.

The tips of Toby's ears turn red. "Sometimes I'm not so sweet. Just ask Pauline. There are days I'm downright grouchy."

"Well, I would be grouchy sometimes to if I was held as a hostage for five years," Shasta says.

Toby's panicked eyes meet mine.

For a moment, I feel awful for sharing his story with the girls. I look at him and try to apologize telepathically.

Toby catches my gaze and shrugs. He takes a deep breath before continuing, "Yeah, it's true. All those years, I was a kidnap survivor made me touchy about certain things. Sometimes, my fear sounds like anger. I don't mean it to be, but that's what happens."

"You call yourself a survivor," Shasta observes. "How long did it take before you felt that way? Right now, I can't help believing it was my fault for falling for his lies."

"Me too," Tiffany adds. "I can't stop kicking myself

for ignoring the voice in the back of my head. My mom is going to be so disappointed. We talked about this a lot when I was younger. Now she's going to think I didn't pay any attention."

"The first thing you need to know is that the man and wife who held you captive and the men you met today are expert manipulators. Their whole goal in life is to make you vulnerable and second-guess your own feelings. They're very good at it. You and Shasta aren't the first victims of Bex Michaels and Felena Hopner. You're just the latest. Hopefully, if we have anything to do with it, you'll be the last."

"What happened to his other victims?" Tiffany asks in a quiet voice.

"I'm friends with a couple of them. It's not always easy, but they are thriving in their new lives. You need to know your life won't be the same because you've gone through something other people have no clue about. However, that doesn't mean it has to rule your life."

Shasta pins Toby with a level stare. "What about the rest of them? It sounds like not everybody is okay."

"I won't lie. Some people have a hard time adjusting. That's what counseling and the people you love are for."

"Oh great! Because of my stupid mistake, I ruined my future," Tiffany grouses.

"Wait! I didn't say that," Toby insists. "Things will be hard for a while, but it doesn't mean you can't be successful. Don't let him rob you of your hopes and dreams. He doesn't deserve that much power."

Shasta takes a drink of her soda. After she carefully sets her glass down, she says, "You're right. He doesn't. But there's still going to be a part of me that hates Bex and Fi Fi."

"It would be strange if you didn't. You're allowed to feel what you feel. It took me a long time to understand that. I thought I needed to be tough and silent. I figured other people didn't need to hear my story. But I'm learning that there's a lot more to me than merely an ex-child hostage."

"I still just want to go home," Tiffany says as her eyes tear up.

"That's what I came to tell you. Tristan chartered private planes for your parents. They'll be here in a couple hours."

"Are you kidding me? Do you know how much those are? Why would he do that?" Shasta demands.

Toby and I look at each other and just snicker. "It's hard to explain. It's just a Tristan thing. Tristan is Toby's boss. He has a thing for planes and since he has developed really famous software and apps, he can afford to fly anybody anywhere — and often does."

"Wow! I want to grow up to be him," Shasta replies.

Toby grins. "It's not outside of the realm of possibility. I messed around with computers when I was a teenager. So, after my brother and his wife rescued me, Identity Bank was my first job."

Tiffany points to the device on my arm. "And now you invent cool things?"

Toby looks a little embarrassed. "I do. Tristan Macklin is the best boss around."

"Pauline said your device is going to be the nail in the coffin for Bex and Fi Fi. You think that's true?" Tiffany asks.

Toby runs his hand through his hair like he always does when he is anxious. "One can only hope."

Shasta nods her head firmly. "Good. I hope they throw away the key. I never want to see them again. In fact, I think I never want to see the whole state of Florida again. Nothing personal — but I didn't have a great time here."

"Me neither, but I don't think it's the fault of the whole state. I'd like to come back and visit Pauline and Toby. I feel like you guys have become friends."

"Well, look at it this way," I answer with a barely disguised grin. "If you don't want to come see us, maybe we can borrow Tristan's plane and visit you instead."

"I'd be totally down with that," Tiffany remarks.

Shasta sits straight up in the booth. "Me too. You guys could come for Mardi Gras."

Toby looks pained. "That many people isn't really my thing. But for you, I'd be willing to give it a shot."

Epilogue

Toby

I LIKE TO TEASE Tristan about his spendthrift ways. But, today I can't even bring myself to be upset. This is going to be the biggest, happiest surprise of Pauline's life and my overly generous boss helped me pull it off.

Pauline snaps her fingers in front of my face. "Are you even paying attention to me? I asked you why you asked me to dress up just so we could put together 3D puzzles in your living room."

"Well, maybe I'm just happy we have things to celebrate. Did I tell you Tiffany's mother sent me a video? She was so grateful. In her eyes, I was the rock star of the op. I know that's not true, but her compliment made me feel like for once I really made a difference."

"Don't feel bad. She made one for our whole department. She even sent over some gourmet coffee and donuts. Cody was grinning from ear to ear all day."

"We really do make a great team, don't we?"

Pauline leans back and snuggles against my chest. "We are amazing together. A force like no other."

I pull her away and turn her so I can see into her eyes.

"Did I ever apologize to you?"

"Why would you need to apologize?"

"I let my fears run away with me and I didn't support you as much as I could've on this operation."

"Are you kidding me? Your messages kept me grounded and in character. Without your help, I might've gone off on Bex Michaels and Felena Hopner. Every time we connected through the device, it reminded me of what was at stake."

I chuckle. "That's very generous of you to say, but I watched you, remember? I know you had the whole operation handled without me."

Pauline is silent for a few moments. "You know, it's weird. This rescue did a great deal to show me my limitations."

"Limitations? You totally kicked the bad guys' butts."

"No. That's not right. We — as in the whole team did it. I liked the feeling of having people watching my back when I couldn't. Maybe you're right, maybe I don't need to charge in like a solo ninja."

"Let me tell you what I learned about you and us. I learned that my fear doesn't have to rule my relationships and I can be supportive even if I am scared."

"That's great news for me. Captain Schumaker is talking about letting me serve at least part-time on the Cold Case Squadron."

"That's totally awesome! After seeing you work with Mariah, Tiffany and Shasta, I understand why he would want you on that team."

Pauline rests her head on my shoulder. "Did I tell you Mariah is going to go home to Alabama after she testifies against Heath Tanner and Oscar Brennan?"

"When did she decide this?" I ask, trying to remember the last time I talked to Mariah.

"Her mom came to support her during the preliminary hearings. She decided that if she was going to testify against her abusers, her mom needed to know the whole story."

"Wow! That's brave of her. I know her two biggest fears were facing Heath again and telling her family what actually happened to her. She is my hero!"

Pauline giggles. "Funny enough, she says the same thing about you because you taught her to be a warrior instead of a victim."

"Is she going to be able to go to school in Alabama?"

Pauline's grin is so bright I almost lose track of the conversation. "That's one of the reasons that she's going back. The University of Alabama offered her a scholarship. She is going to major in criminal justice. She's talking about someday going to law school. Isn't that something?"

"Since you give me credit for encouraging her to be a warrior, you have to take some credit here too. One of the reasons she believes she can do any of that stuff is because you have been such a good friend and role model for her."

Pauline's face flushes. "I guess that's just one more example of how we are an unstoppable team. I'm so proud of her."

"You don't suppose she needs a fully decked out truck for college or anything, do you?" I tease.

"No, that would be a little much. But knowing

Tristan, he's probably going to give her a car as a bon voyage gift anyway."

I laugh out loud. "No doubt — you know, because he's Tristan."

When the doorbell rings, we both jump. Pauline looks at me with a confused expression. "Did you order pizza or something? We just ate."

"I dunno. Let's go see who it is." I grab her hand and pull her up off the couch. Sliding my arm around her waist, we walk toward my front door.

When I open it, Pauline shrieks with delight. "Mom and Dad? What are you doing here?" Her parents step aside to reveal my parents. "Bonnie and Wesley? Okay, if I was surprised to see my parents, I'm totally shocked to see you. You live in Oregon, right?"

"We do," my mom says as she gives Pauline a big hug. "But we heard it was your birthday. So, we couldn't miss the party."

I arch an eyebrow at Toby. "Just a quiet night working on puzzles, huh? How did you do this? My birthday isn't even until Tuesday."

My dad is carrying a big box. He sets it down on the kitchen table and slowly takes something out of it.

"What's that?" Pauline asks as she watches his progress.

Pauline gasps when she sees the birthday cake in the shape of the lid of her dress blues.

I stop dead in my tracks when I see the logo on the box. "Only a cake from Joy and Tiers, the best bakery on the West Coast! How in the world did you guys get this through security?"

My mom appears at my side and kisses me on the cheek. "Who said we went through security? Did you know your boss has his own plane?"

Pauline and I bust up laughing. "Score one for Tristan," she says as she dips her finger in the frosting and tastes it. "Oh my gosh! No wonder you don't want to leave Oregon. If I had this bakery in my neighborhood, I would eat there every day."

"I don't understand why you're laughing, I thought what your boss did was extraordinarily nice," my mom says with a puzzled expression.

"That's just the thing, Bonnie — it was profoundly nice. Tristan is so generous, sometimes he makes our head spin. We never know when he's going to strike again."

"So, son, have you made a decision about where you're going to work?" my dad asks.

"Why don't you have a seat in the living room. This could take a while."

I see Pauline blanch. "Don't assume it's bad news," I murmur in her year.

She visibly relaxes. "You guys want anything to eat or drink?"

"No thank you. We're good," my mom answers.

Pauline looks at her parents. "Dad, want a cup of coffee?"

Desmond sets his crutch down as he sits down beside his wife. "Not especially. I'm more interested in the answer to the question posed to your beau."

"I'm trying not to cry, but I need to know too," Pauline says as she sits down beside her dad.

I walk over and stand in front of Pauline. "So, you all know I worked on a special project with Tristan and Identity Bank to help keep Pauline alive during her latest op."

Christie nods. "There aren't enough words in the English language to thank you for all you did to keep our daughter safe."

"Well, it turns out there are a variety of agencies and companies which would like to adopt the technology. Some of them are related to the military, but other applications include keeping senior citizens safe when they don't have access to a phone. But my favorite idea for the invention is to develop it for at-risk kids such as those with profound autism. Potentially, it could cut down on the number of kids who are lost."

"That's just amazing! We are so proud of you son," my mom says.

"And … What does that mean for your job?" Pauline asks.

"Tristan wants me here in Florida to be on the development team. He wants to make sure investors understand the proprietary software and its potential uses."

Pauline jumps up and gives me a huge hug. "So this means you're staying? You're really, really, really staying?"

I laugh at her enthusiasm. "Yes, I'm really staying. You'll have one more citizen to protect."

"You know I would take bullets for you because I love you," Pauline announces without any hesitation.

I grin. "I'm aware. I've seen you in action. Although, anyone around you might have a hard time holding onto a gun."

"You are so funny."

"What's he talking about, honey? I have a feeling you didn't tell me everything about this op," Desmond says.

I shoot a surprised glance over at Desmond. "Oh, Pauline didn't tell you? She single-handedly disarmed the bad guy using the techniques you taught her."

"I didn't want to brag, Dad. We talked about this. I'm trying to fly under the radar."

"Approaching your job with caution doesn't mean you can't be proud when you take down a perp."

My dad gives Desmond a thumbs up. "Amen to that!"

I nervously stick my hand in my pocket and then kneel in front of Pauline.

"I have one more question. Pauline, when we met, I had deep scars on my soul. I wasn't even sure I would ever trust anyone enough to fall in love — but with you it was different. I fell completely and totally in love with you and with myself in the process. You see my soul scars, but let me work through them. Earlier, we were talking about what a great team we make. So, I'm asking you to be my teammate for life. Pauline Christine Lawrence, will you marry me?"

Tears are running down Pauline's face. "Oh my gosh! This definitely isn't building puzzles on the coffee room table. I worried that I would never find someone who loves me for me even though I always stick my foot in my mouth and leap before I look."

"So … That's a yes?" I ask as my heart about beats out of my chest.

She pulls me up to my feet and throws her arms

around my neck. "Yes! I want to be your teammate and soulmate forever."

I gently take her shaking hand and place an engagement ring on her finger.

"I can't believe this! You got me a purple ring! I love it. It is so me."

"It is unique and lovely just like you. I couldn't have your engagement ring clash with your usual hair accessories."

Christie turns to my mom. "Bonnie, can you imagine how much fun we're going to have planning this wedding?"

Bonnie nods. "It's going to be a blast. I have a feeling your daughter is going to be anything but a typical bride."

Pauline looks up at me with a misty-eyed grin. "You realize we've just lost complete control of our wedding, don't you?"

"I don't care as long as the day makes you happy."

"I have a vision of a field of daisies," my mom suggests.

"That would make me very happy," Pauline announces. "Hey, I just thought of something. I'm going to be Detective Payne. That ought to be amusing enough to Cody that he'll stop calling me Rookie."

Desmond chokes back a laugh. "My training officer is seventy-five years old and he still calls me The Rookie. Doesn't seem to bother him that I'm retired. I'm sorry to tell you, you'll have that label forever."

"Works for me. As long as I am next to this guy, they can call me whatever they want."

Epilogue

Pauline

I HIKE MY DEEP purple evening gown up far enough to get into Toby's vehicle.

He grins when he sees the flash of my leg. "I should've taken Tristan's advice and kept his truck. I didn't realize truck ownership had such wonderful perks."

"You're so funny! Isn't your new truck pretty much identical to the one you gave to Hope's Haven?"

I nod. "If anything, I think it has a few more bells and whistles. But the difference is I'm buying this one on my own because I earned it."

"I say you did. Your technology saved three lives in its debut outing. You can't ask for much more than that."

"I know. But Tristan didn't have to give me a raise. I did it as part of my job."

"I know, but here's the thing — when you do a great job, your employer has the right to compensate you for what they think it's worth."

"You're mighty effusive with your compliments. Let's see how you feel when the shoe is on the other foot Ms. 'I'm getting an award for valor from the mayor.'"

I reach up and touch the device attached to my upper arm. "You're right, I'll probably be just as uncomfortable when they talk about how good I am. I still can't believe I'm being singled out. It wasn't just me. The whole team deserves to be recognized."

Toby reaches out and strokes the back of my hand. "Sometimes, being the youngest detective on the team and scoring a huge bust of pedophiles means you get to be featured front and center. You once told me that you wanted to be known for changing the world. You have done just that and you deserve all the praise."

"Tiffany's right. You are the sweetest man on the planet. I'm so glad you love me."

I have a sense of déjà vu as I enter the ballroom. The last time I was here, I was sure Toby and I were done forever. What a difference a year makes!

I gasp when I look up and see the same waiter who was so generous to us last time.

"Can I escort you to your seats?" he offers as he sticks his elbow out for me.

"So much for hiding in the back of the room," I murmur.

The waiter chuckles. "I think you'll like these seats. They were specially chosen for you."

When we reach the table, I almost trip in surprise. "What are you guys doing here?"

"Did you think we were going to let you face this crowd alone?" Shasta replies.

Tiffany pulls up a strap on her dress that fell over her shoulder. "Yeah, we couldn't do that. You had our backs when we needed you the most. So, we came here to tell everyone how much you mean to us and how grateful we are that you not only saved our lives, but you've become our friend."

"Isn't she the greatest? Pauline was the first person who believed in me when I couldn't believe in myself. Without her, my life would be much different," Mariah says. "I'm so proud to be following in her footsteps. I just hope I can be half the cop she is."

Suddenly, Cody starts hitting his glass on the stage.

"Have I got everyone's attention?"

The crowd murmurs.

"So, I don't know what it is about my partners, they just tend to take heroic to a whole new level. Twice in two years, the two best partners I've ever had have been honored for their passionate police work. So, playing the odds it's my turn next year, right?"

The audience laughs.

"No, seriously. I love being a training officer because I get to meet the brightest, most talented cops who are the future of our force. I may be prejudiced, but I have to tell you, Officer Lawrence is one of the most talented cops I've ever worked with. She outthinks, outworks and out-hustles anyone else on the force."

I dab away tears at his praise. I have spent my career trying to live up to his high standards. There were times, I never thought I would meet them.

Cody sees my response and starts to tear up too. He clears his throat and continues, "When Pauline first came to us, I called her Rookie. Even though it's been several years, her nickname hasn't changed. But tonight, I want to let you all know that I am darn proud to call Detective Lawrence my partner and friend. She's no rookie — she's a bona fide hero."

I mouth the words thank you to Cody.

He smiles. "You don't have to thank me. There's a whole collection of people here who want to thank you for your service. I'm just happy to be part of Team Lawrence."

I squeeze Toby's hand. "I don't know if I can handle a whole night of this."

Toby whispers in my ear, "Cody is right, you know. The smartest thing I ever did was join your team. You changed my life and I will love you forever."

NOTE FROM THE AUTHOR

Dear Reader,

Dear Reader,

Thank you for reading my books. If you love characters with unique challenges and big hearts, you'll love The Heart of Summer

Joe Summers gave his heart to a woman once. It didn't go well.

He thought she would be there forever, she thought he was good for some fun and games.

Not only did she break off their engagement, she left him to raise their son.

Now his son has fallen in love with a beautiful charming woman. The little guy has decided Brynley should be his mom.

How does he explain to his son that simply choosing someone to love doesn't mean they want to stay in your life.

Soul Scars

If you love sweet romance with a hint of mystery,
The Heart of Summer is for you.

Coming Winter of 2019

~Mary

Because love matters, differences don't.

ACKNOWLEDGMENTS

THIS BOOK WAS AN especially difficult book to write. In all the headlines regarding sexual assault, it's often easy to forget that many victims our children — and those children include boys.

I wish to thank everyone who has bravely shared their story with me about the ongoing trauma being a victim induces. I tried to tell the story as honestly as possible even when it hurt.

I have a team of people to thank.

A special thank you to recently, my editor. You always push me to be crisper, cleaner and more direct. My books are better because of you.

To Kathern Watts, I don't know what I would do without you. You are my encyclopedia of knowledge about all of my characters. Thank for all of your help.

Lacey, thank you for making sure people know about my books. If you weren't in my life, and will be much less organized and visible.

Thank you to my beta readers for catching the mistakes and identifying things that don't make sense.

Kathy McGee, thank you for your brilliant work on my new covers. It's like you crawled into my imagination and pulled out exactly what I envisioned. I can't tell you how much I appreciate your work.

Christina Bergmann, as always, your keen eye for details made my book better.

Finally, I need to say word about the never-ending support I receive from my husband, Leonard Crawford. Even during the scary times, you are forever my cheerleader and sounding board. I love you.

To my kids Justin and Brandon, thank you for sharing your expertise with me. It helps make my books make sense.

ABOUT THE AUTHOR

I have been lucky enough to live my own version of a romance novel. I married the guy who kissed me at summer camp. He told me on the night we met that he was going to marry me and be the father of my children.

Eventually, I stopped giggling when he said it, and we've been married for more than thirty years. We have two children. The oldest is a Doctor of Osteopathy. He is across the United States completing his residency, but when he's done, he is going to come back to Oregon and practice Family Medicine. Our youngest son is now tackling high school and where he is an honor student. He is interested in becoming an EMT.

I write full time now. I have published more than thirty books and have several more underway. I volunteer my time to a variety of causes. I have worked as a Civil Rights Attorney and diversity advocate. I spent several years working for various social service agencies before becoming an attorney.

In my spare time, I love to cook, decorate cakes and of course, I obsessively, compulsively read.

I would be honored if you would take a few moments out of your busy day to check out my website,

MaryCrawfordAuthor.com. While you're there, you can sign up for my newsletter and get a free book. I will be announcing my upcoming books and giving sneak peeks as well as sponsoring giveaways and giving you information about other interesting events.

If you have questions or comments, please E-mail me at Mary@MaryCrawfordAuthor.com or find me on the following social networks:

Facebook: www.facebook.com/authormarycrawford

Website: MaryCrawfordAuthor.com

Twitter: www.twitter.com/MaryCrawfordAut

www.ingramcontent.com/pod-product-compliance
Lightning Source LLC
Chambersburg PA
CBHW050522190726
48284CB00003B/913